Books by Leonard Michaels

Going Places (1969)
I Would Have Saved Them If I Could (1975)
The Men's Club (1981)
Shuffle (1990)

Shuffle

SHUFFLE

Leonard

Michaels

Michael di Capua Books

Farrar, Straus and Giroux

New York

For Raquel

Contents

Journal

§ Sobbing like a child, he phoned his wife at her lover's apartment. She had to ask him to repeat himself.

"I want you to come home and collect your clothes."

She'd been conscious of his pain before then, but in a general way. To her lover, she'd confessed, "I feel guilty for not feeling guilty." She could virtually see her dresses and shoes in the bedroom closet. She hurried home. Her husband locked the door and beat her up. "Did you do it with him in the toilet?" He forced her to do it there with him, too. The same for every room in the house. "It really happened," she said, laughing at herself. "It saved my marriage. You'd think I could write about that."

We reviewed the events. She told her husband about the other man and named him. Already, to my mind, a failed marriage. Her husband should have known her body, guessed there was another man. Smells change with metallic brilliance in erotic chemistry. Besides, her love affair should have reached him in how she gave herself. "Where did you learn to do that?" He never asked.

He made nothing of her luminous moods or impatience with him. "How many times have I told you to put the cap back on the toothpaste tube?" Even her revulsion at the shape of his feet didn't strike him as a curious development. She imitated him muttering, shaking his head: "That's how they always looked." He made nothing of his own malaise. Simply didn't know why he'd become that way. He'd had to be told about her lover. The poor man's suffering exceeded his understanding. He beat her up.

"But it really happened," she said again, laughing moronically at herself. "Maybe I'll try to write it as a poem."

Another woman at the literary conference, drawn forth by the story, said her husband accused her of sleeping with his best friend. The accusations, beginning at breakfast, resumed at night when he returned from work. He ruined her nicest dinners. He ruined her sleep. All her efforts to make them happy—she "really tried" —were turned ugly by his suspiciousness. Marriage counseling did no good. Her husband wouldn't discuss "real problems."

"Were you?" I asked.

"What?"

"Fucking his friend?"

"Yes, but that's not the point."

She lifted her hands, fingers bent to mean hard labor.

"I cleaned. I cooked. I washed his filthy hairs out of the bathtub."

There was nothing anyone could say.

In the emptiness, I remembered how I used to meet a woman, on Sunday mornings, behind her church. I waited in my car, in the shade of a low-hanging willow, until the service was over. Then she would appear, striking across the steamy asphalt of the parking lot in her high heels and dark blue churchgoing suit, a white flower in the lapel. She looked magnificent, yet my car was good enough; all we needed. As she talked of God, her cloud of hair floated in a blonder light. Once she surprised me, her voice reproachful, as if I'd done something bad. But it was her fiancé, not me. She said he'd made a gruesome scene, shrieking at her in a crowded oyster bar, "You sucked another man's cock."

I started to kiss her. She thrust me back, making me see how pity mixed with pain in her eyes. "Can you believe he said that to me? All those people sitting there eating oysters. Can you imagine how I felt?" I nodded yes, yes, needing to kiss her, but she wanted me to wait, to let the sacred fullness of her sorrow sink into me. She wanted me to feed on her immensely beseeching stare, prim blue suit, little flower in the lapel. I pressed her backward. She tucked up her skirt. Slick thighs flashed in the shady car. The pretty church danced beyond the willow. Her fiancé, far away, suffering . . . It should matter, but in the pitch of things there is no should.

"You're greedy," she said.

I asked her to marry me.

Her lips moved against my cheek, as if I were a deaf child, each word a touching pressure. "You know," she whispered, "I've never gotten a speeding ticket. The cop looks at me and can't seem to write it. When they start writing me tickets, ask again."

She saved me from myself, but why did I want her? She was only ten years older than my son. He'd have started smoking dope; run away.

"Can you believe my fiancé said that to me?"

Her question passed like the shadow of a bird through my heart.

§ Beard wrote to me saying he'd heard there was "bad blood" between us. We'd met only two or three times. There was hardly anything between us. I wrote back, impelled by guilt, though I could imagine nothing to feel guilty about. Then came the phone calls. We tried to make a date for lunch. He didn't want to come to Berkeley. I didn't want to go to San Francisco. He said if he came to Berkeley, I'd pay for lunch. If I came to San Francisco, he'd pay. Again guilt. Which did he prefer? I couldn't tell. I said I'd go to him. It was difficult to find a place to park, then I had to walk five blocks to his apartment house. I felt I was paying for something. He answered the door with a letter in his hand. Irrationally,

I supposed it was for me. On our way out to lunch, he said it was a letter of condolence to the wife of a friend, a famous writer, who had just died. He said it was easy for him to write the letter, having had to write so many of them lately. He flipped it into a mailbox. We ate in a local restaurant. He left the table several times to talk to women at other tables and the bar. Walking back to his apartment, he told me about a time when he didn't write a letter of condolence to the wife. He didn't like her, he said. Her husband, his good friend, had also been a famous writer. She'd been sexually unfaithful to him with his friends. She taunted him with it, made him feel despised and lonely. Finally he died. Soon afterwards, she phoned Beard and asked why he hadn't written her a letter. It was the middle of the night. She was drunk. She raved about the many letters of condolence she had received. Everybody of importance in the literary world had written her. Why not Beard? I thought it was a good story and asked if I could have it. He looked puzzled. He hadn't thought the story was anything special. Now he wondered. He was reluctant to say I could have it. Again guilt: I had enjoyed the story too much, understanding more than he intended. I'd seen the woman raving drunkenly into the phone at Beard. I supposed he'd fucked her, but that wasn't interesting. I was seeing her pain. At his apartment we had a drink. Then, as we stood together in the narrow hallway to his door, saying goodbye, assuring each other there was no bad blood, he farted. The tight space became noxiously suffocating. Eager to get out, I said for perhaps the third time, "There is no bad blood." He said, as though it hadn't ever really mattered, "A puff of smoke."

§ Jimmy sits at his typewriter high on cocaine, smiling, shaking his head. He says, "I'm so good I don't even have to write." He's six foot three and charcoal brown, the color of a Burmese cat. His chest is high and wide. From neck to belt he is a hard, flat wall. No hips. Apple ass. Long legs. Long hands and feet. He looks as good in clothes as he looks naked. In both senses, clothes *become* his body. A woman said he is so clearly a man he could wear a dress. He sits at his typewriter, smiling, shaking his head. There is nothing wrong with him. He doesn't even have to write.

§ Evelyn had something to tell me, needed my opinion, I must come right away. She said she had met a famous writer. "He got the Pulitzer Prize." I say that's nice, so what? She says he asked her to do something. I say what? She can't say. Oh, come on. Really, what? I know you want to tell me, so tell me. "Please," she begs. "Please don't do this to me. You're my friend. I feel soiled. It was so disgusting." She drops her head, takes her hair in her fists. I say what? what? what? She just can't say it. Suddenly she screams, "I mean I was flattered, but he's over seventy. He told me to phone him when I go East this Christmas, he's in the National Academy, the Hall of Fame, everything, but what should I do? Tell him I'm pregnant? I'll say, 'Your friendship means more to me than anything, but I'm pregnant, I can't do it, I'm liable to vomit. I can't even look at a pizza.' "

§ Kafka imagines a man who has a hole in the back of his head. The sun shines into this hole. The man himself is denied a glimpse of it. Kafka might as well be talking about the man's face. Others "look into it." The most public, promiscuous part of his body is invisible to himself. How obvious. Still, it takes a genius to say that what kisses, sneezes, whistles, and moans is a hole more private than our privates. You retreat from it into quotidian blindness, the blindness of your face to itself. You want to light a cigarette or fix yourself a drink. You want to make a phone call. To whom? You don't know. Of course you don't. You want to phone your face. The one you've never met. Who you are.

§ Jimmy says he met a woman at a literary conference in Miami. They spent the night talking and smoking marijuana in his hotel room. They read their stories to each other. He says he had a great time. Never touched once. The talk was so good. Later it came to him—he doesn't know why—the woman is a man. He saw her the next day. He wanted to ask but he couldn't think how to put it. "Hey, man, are you a man?" Either way, her feelings would be hurt. He snaps his fingers, claps, says, "That is the trouble with women, you dig?"

§ Plato says the face is a picture of the soul. Could this be true? I thought how noses, teeth, ears, and eyes—in the faces of Evelyn's ancestors—flowing through the centuries, once combined in a certain way to make the picture of her soul, until she had her teeth fixed and her ears pinned back. But a face is more like a word than like a picture. It has an etymology. Ancient meanings, drawn from the peculiarities of races, geography, weather, flora, fauna, war, and love, collect in a face as in a word. ("The face that launched a thousand ships.") In Evelyn's face, I saw the travels of Marco Polo, the fall of Constantinople, the irredentist yearnings of Hungaro-Romanians. Doctor, how many thousands vanished when Evelyn had her teeth fixed? In Evelyn's face I saw the hordes of Genghis Khan racing toward Europe, among them a yellow brute, with a long thin mustache flowing away from his nostrils like black ribbons and streaming along either side of his mouth, who raped Evelyn's great-great-great-grandmother with his fierce prick, thereby giving to Evelyn's cheekbones a distinctly slanted plane, her nicest feature.

——

§ I'm in Boris's living room. He fixed me a drink. We sit in chairs facing each other. His girlfriend prepares dinner. I'm grateful for the comfort, the prospect of dinner with them. I've brought a bottle of wine, but it's hardly enough. I must give of myself, something personal, something real. None of us has long enough to live for yet another civilized conversation. Boris waits, enjoying the wine. He looks peaceful. Perhaps the book he is writing is going well, but I don't ask. A book is a tremendous project of excruciating difficulty; sacred business. Thomas Mann lit candles before he began to write. Kafka imagined huge spikes below his desktop which would drive into his knees. To ask Boris if his book is going well would be like asking if he writes with a pencil or a pen. I tell Boris I'm still working on the screenplay. I hope that makes him feel good, superior to me. A screenplay is a low order of writing, nothing compared to a book. He says, "Don't be ashamed. Movies are the most important art form of our day." As always, he's brilliantly penetrating. I am embarrassed, confused. I wanted to say something real and offered a species of fraudulence. He saw through it instantly. But I can't stop now. I tell him the work is torture, hours and hours of typing, though it is relieved by flights to New York and L.A., fine hotels and good restaurants, the company of celebrities, actors, whores.

Boris says, "I don't want to hear about it."

The pleasant noise from the kitchen, where his girlfriend cooks, comes to a stop. She overheard us. Women have superb ears. In the deepest sleep, they can hear a baby crying. She appears in the living room, saying, "We're going to have the most delicious crab that ever lived."

I say, "What do you mean you don't want to hear about it?"

She says, "Boris only means . . ." but he raises his hand, cuts her short. Then he says, "I just don't want to, that's all. Fuck it."

I'm yelling now, "Well, what the fuck do you want to hear about?"

"How about my book?" he shouts. "You never fucking ask about my book."

§ The woman started doing it again, scratching at her neck. It was difficult to ignore. I tried to look elsewhere, but I lectured in confusion and finally dismissed the class early. Amid the rush of students, I stopped her.

"Miss Toiler, do you notice how students chew gum and writhe in their seats?"

"You must see everything."

"I do," I said, pressing her with my look, willing her to leap from the general to the particular. I stood close to her, too close, but she appeared comfortable, receptive, and looked back at me. Her blue eyes were light as her hair, the pupils dark and flat. Her hair was exceptionally fine, several shades below blond. Something in me grew still, gazing, desiring nothing. She was in her late twenties, older than most of my students. The class was gone now, the hallway empty. I could speak to the point.

"You're not from California, are you?"

Thus, no point. I changed the subject I never raised, then asked if she'd like to have coffee.

"We arrived this summer," she said. "My husband took a job with an engineering firm in Palo Alto." Her gray wool suit and black shoes were wrong for the hot September morning. Her creamy silk blouse, also too warm, was sealed high on her neck by a cameo, obscuring scratches she had inflicted on herself. She looked correct in an East Coast way, insulated by propriety.

"Stanton is a geologist and an engineer."

I imagined a tall Stanton, then no—average height, or maybe a short man with a lust for power, or, like her black shoes, officious and priestly. I knew nothing. My mind swung around the periphery of concern, like my spoon in the coffee cup.

"Do you have children?"

"I have horses." Smiling, lips together, showing no teeth. Her horses were special, delicious. She blushed, an emotional phenomenon long vanished from this world. It embarrassed me. She said she loved to ride in the hills after dinner. She'd once seen a bobcat. Her voice lifted. The memory excited her. I smiled consciously, trying to seem pleased.

"In Palo Alto?"

She giggled. "We live far from any town."

She didn't scratch at her neck, but occasionally pushed her knuckles at her nose. She had long, tapering, spiritual fingers. Her skirt, tight-fitting, showed the line of her thigh, good athletic legs.

"I should tell you that I'll be missing some classes. I have to go to doctors' appointments."

"Nothing serious, I hope."

"I might have a tropical parasite. Nigerian fluke. We lived in Africa for a year while Stanton worked for an oil company." She smiled again in the prissy way. Telling about the fluke presumed too much. "It's probably an allergy. All the new grasses and flowers. The Bay Area is a hotbed of allergies. Stanton loved Africa. He doesn't blame me for ruining things. I had a persistent fever. Poor Stanton quit the job because of me. He's so good. Very healthy. He lifts weights." She grinned, shrugged.

At the south gate, we said goodbye. I went to my office. There was a knock, then Henry peeked in. "Busy?" He carried an unlit cigarette. I waved him inside. He sat; lit his cigarette. His head, fixed high on a skinny neck, was eagle-like; critical. "What's new?" he said.

"I have a student who tears at her neck while I lecture. What should I do?"

"I never thought of you as squeamish."

"I'm not squeamish."

"I would tell you about an extremely offensive student, but you won't believe me."

"Yes, I will."

"If you repeat it, I'll say it's a lie. There's a gentleman in my class—a Mr. Woo—who has a mandarin fingernail."

"No shit."

"On the little finger of his left hand, the nail is ten inches long. It's a symbol of his leisurely life."

"You find his fingernail extremely offensive?"

"Why should I care about his fingernail? His face is a mass of pus pimples and he grins at me throughout the hour, as if everything I say is intended for him."

"He's in love with you."

"I want to throw a knife through his face. There's a pilot in my class who is an alcoholic. All pilots, surgeons, and judges are drunks. You know this is true?"

"Everyone knows."

Henry stood, turned to the door.

After the next class, Toiler waited outside the room, leaning against a wall, pretending to read her notes. She wore the same suit with a white shirt and a thin black tie. She looked boyish, ascetic, pretty.

"Would you like to have coffee? I'll buy it this time."

I couldn't remember saying yes.

As we talked, she didn't touch her face or neck. Had I cured her by seeming flirtatious? Sexual juices have healing power. I'd intended nothing, but the human face, with its probing looks and receptive smiles, is a sexual organ. I wondered if Toiler, scratching at her neck, yearned only to be touched.

She said, "I won't be able to meet you after class next time. I go to my doctor."

I hadn't asked her to meet me.

She missed the next class and the next and the next.

Maybe I was glad not to see her, but I didn't wonder. I simply forgot her. Over the years whole classes go from memory, as if you'd been lecturing to nobody, hallucinating in the flow of academic seasons. Thales, the first philosopher, said everything is water. I remembered Thales as I stared out my office window at the black-green trees of the Berkeley hills and the glaring blue of a cloudless sky. A hawk circled, invoked by some bird or mouse, generating flirtatious signals.

The term was half over when I found Toiler waiting outside my office. "I must talk about dropping the class," she said.

I ushered her inside, gesturing toward the chair. She wore a new suit, summery cotton, lavender with a dull sheen. Its vitality suggested compromise with California. The dark green silk of her blouse had the lush solemnity of a rain forest. It lay open negligently, not casually, revealing a bra strap and scratches on her neck, like spears of thin red grass slanted this way and that by an uncertain wind. She wasn't cured.

"I thought you'd dropped the class."

"It's the doctors' appointments. They can't tell me anything. All they do is give me different drugs. Can I take the class independently? I'll make up the work, do the reading on my own, and write a paper."

A breeze, from the slightly open window behind her, pressed the back of her neck. She shivered.

"Are you uncomfortable? Move away from the window."

"I'm fine," she said.

"Independent study means conferences. Driving back and forth. Hours on the highway."

"I want to do it." She was resigned to the highway, resigned to sit shivering.

The spasms became stronger. Her torn neck demanded attention. Was it a plea for help? Students in my office sometimes cried over disaffected boyfriends, alcoholic parents, suicidal roommates. I stood up and stepped to the window, knowing I wanted only to shut her blouse. The window was built in an old, luxurious style, plenty of oak and glass. I pulled. It moved a little, then stuck, fused in its runners.

"Please don't bother," she said.

Her face, close to my right hip, looked dismayed and apologetic, with sweet pre-Raphaelite melancholy, otherworldly, faintly morbid. Her husband didn't blame her for ruining things. I could see why. Dreamy hair, eyes of a snow leopard, lacerated neck. I felt pity, not blame; frustration more than pity. The window wouldn't move. Then fingers slid beneath the sash. To pull from the bottom. Ethereal fingers vanished as sixty pounds of wood and glass rushed down. Smashed them. She gasped. I lunged, shoving the window back up, the strength of gorillas suddenly in my arms. "I'm so sorry,"

I said, backing away. She whispered, "My fault, my fault," her eyes lit by weird, apologetic glee. "I did it. It's my own fault."

Her hands lay palms up in her lap, fingers greenish-blue. They looked dead, a memory of hands. I sat, waiting for it to end. Turgid feeling, like the walls of a tomb, enclosed us. I said, "Drop the course. Take it independently. Do it any way you like."

She whispered, "Don't you care what I do?"

"What do you mean?"

"You know."

"I do?"

"You started this."

"This?"

"Yes, this."

"What? You sit there shivering in front of me. I go to the window. You stick your hands under it . . ."

She leaned forward and kicked me in the shin. Her green blouse, with its open collar, looked more dissolute than negligent; the torn neck fierce. Her posture stiffened, as if she carried a bowl of indignation within. Abruptly she reached to her purse, snapping it open. She removed a pearly comb and pulled it through her hair swiftly. Her hands were all right. She stopped, glanced at me, startled, remembering where she was.

"May I?" she said.

"Go ahead."

Long, gleaming tears flowed from her eyes, in the way

of a child too deeply hurt to make a sound. She combed her hair. I watched. She finished, put the comb back into her purse, snapped it shut, and walked to the door in three brisk steps, as if she had somewhere to go. Books and papers lay on my desk in a meaningless clutter. I put them in order as the office darkened.

The next day I received a note on heavy beige paper, in a fine, small, careful handwriting. It said she'd dropped all classes, apologized for wasting my time, and thanked me for being patient. Squeezed into the right corner was a phone number. I read the note twice, looking for more than it said. The clear script, with its even pressure, said nothing inadvertently. I folded it, put it into my pocket, then picked up the phone. I was about to do something I'd regret, but after dialing I only listened to ringing, monotonous ringing. I phoned her from my office, gas stations, drugstores, restaurants . . .

One afternoon, on the way out to lunch with Henry, I said, "A student of mine who lived in Africa came back with a parasite. She calls it Nigerian fluke. Have you heard of it?"

"Nigerian fluke is fatal in every case. I've had many students who were diseased . . ."

"She dropped out."

"See?" Henry seized my elbow and stopped me, grinning as if pleased, yet frightened. "But I'm not a doctor," he said. "And I've never been right about anything. She's dead?"

"Dropped out. That's all I know."

As we left the building, he asked, "Were you smitten by her?"

The daylight was so pure there seemed nothing to say. Like creatures sliding into a lake without disturbing the surface, we entered it.

§ I visited a monastery in the wilderness. The monks had carved every stone by hand. It took years to complete. They were content, but their work was so ugly it seemed to comment on their faith. I wandered in halls and courtyard looking for a redeeming touch. There was none. In works of self-abnegating faith is there necessary ugliness?

§ In the American South, it's said of a medical student, "He is going to make a doctor." For writers there is no comparable expression, no diploma, no conclusive evidence that anything real has been made of himself or herself.

§ I go to the movies. The hero's girlfriend, about twenty years younger than he, tells him that he is made stupid by his closeness to realities such as work, debts, domestic life. He sees too clearly the little daily facts. He lacks historical understanding, the perspective required for political action. She berates him because he doesn't assassinate the President, blow up a department store, change the world. He sits stolidly in his tweed jacket and dark knit tie. The seriousness of his expression tells me that he suffers, like a European intellectual, the moral weight of thought. He has no choice. The scriptwriter gave him nothing to say in defense of himself. I want to shout for him, "What do you know, you narcissistic bitch with your bullshit Marxism and five-hundred-dollar shoes from Paris," etc. But she is good-looking. I grow quiet inside and try to take in her whole meaning. I wonder, if she were plain, would I put up with her for a minute? The hero wants to be a good man, think the right thoughts, do the right things. I believe he wants more to shove his face between her legs. The scriptwriter is no fool. Why should he give the hero anything to say? It's enough to sustain a serious expression. This is like life, but I think I can't stand it another minute, when suddenly she collapses into feeling and says she wants his baby; that is, she wants him to give her a baby. They lie down on a narrow couch, still wearing their clothes, him in his oppressive tweed jacket, which probably stinks of cigarettes. He is presumably giving her a baby as the scene fades. Is this also like life? Or is the question whether any drama exists without irrationality at the center? *King Lear*, the greatest drama, is greatest in irrationality from start to finish. Oh, come off it. The question is, When did I last do it with my clothes on? My senior year in high school? No, I remember a hard, cold, dirty floor, papers strewn about, and a shock of hot wet flesh through clothing, wintry light in the windows, the radiator banging, a draft from beneath the door sliding across my ass, the telephone ringing, voices outside saying, "He isn't here." "Knock." "I knocked, he isn't here." And the indifference to all that in her eyes, their yellowish-brown gaze taking me into her feelings. She said, "Wait for me. I have to go to the bathroom." How real that seemed, its sensational banality. My hands trembled, making the flame jerk when I tried to light my cigarette. Why did I light it? Was it a way of collecting the minutes we'd lost? She straightened her skirt, and then, with a quick wiggle, hoisted her pants. Odd not to have straightened her skirt last, but like her. "What are you laughing at, you?" she said.

§ Ortega says men are public, women are private. Montaigne says if you want to know all about me, read my book. "My book has made me," says Montaigne, "as much as I made it." In the same spirit, a man writes a letter, then decides not to mail it. He thinks it's himself, a great letter, too good for just one person. It should be published. One of Byron's letters was made into a poem. Real intimacy is for the world, not a friend.

§ The woman wakes beside me and tells me her dream. She might forget otherwise. Nothing is easier to forget than a dream, or more difficult to remember. Her voice —I'm half asleep—twists into my skull, trailing a residue of strange events. This is always irritating, but I wake, listen, urge her to see more, see the whole dream. Frightening, sad, funny, her voice remains neutral, as if it mustn't interfere with what she sees. The secret of writing.

§ Writers die twice, first their bodies, then their works, but they produce book after book, like peacocks spreading their tails, a gorgeous flare of color soon shlepped through the dust.

§ I phoned my mother. She said, "You sound happy. What's the matter?"

§ They say "Hi" and kiss my cheek as if nothing terrible happened yesterday. Perhaps they have no memory of anything besides money or sex, so they harbor no grudges and live only for action. "What's up?" Just pleasure, distractions from anxiety and boredom. Impossible to sustain conversation with them for more than forty seconds. The attention span of dogs. Everything must be up. They say you look great when you look near death. They laugh at jokes you didn't make. They say you're brilliant when you're confused and stupid.

§ I phoned Boris. He's sick. He gets tired quickly, can't think, can't work. I asked if he'd like to take a walk in the sun. He cries, "It's a nice day out there. I know it, believe me."

§ Feelings come for no reason. I'm tyrannized by them. I see in terms of them until they go away. Also for no reason.

§ Bodega Bay. Want to write, but I sit for hours looking at the dune grass. It is yellow-green and sun-bleached. It sparkles and changes hue with the changing light. It is more hue than color, like the whole northern coast. Now the dune grass has the sheen of fur. I need to be blind.

§ Anything you say to a writer is in danger of becoming writing.

§ The poets reading their poems.

The critics reading their criticism.

The him reading his me.

The Cedar River, the woods, the fields.

I prefer the houses and barns of Iowa to what *knows* it prefers.

§ Boris tells me, apropos of nothing, that he has been rereading certain novels and poems. It's as if he is talking to himself, yet he is curious to hear my opinion. He says the novels and poems mean different things whenever he returns to them. As he talks, he picks up a small lacquered bowl which he brought back from Japan. It is very old, very good. It has the aura of a museum object whose value has emerged over time and declared itself absolutely, but he studies it with a worried, skeptical, suspicious eye.

§ Dinner party. Mrs. R. kept asking Z how her son got into Harvard, as if it had nothing to do with his gifts. Z laughed, virtually apologizing, though she's very proud of her son, who is a good kid and also a genius, which I tried to suggest, but Mrs. R. wouldn't hear it because her son didn't get into Harvard and she was too miserable or drunk merely to agree that Z's son would be welcome at any university. Mr. R. left the table, went to the piano, and started banging Haydn on the keys so nobody could hear his wife raving about Harvard, but she raised her voice and talked about her glorious days in graduate school when she took seminars with Heidegger and then she asked Z, "When exactly did you stop loving *your* kids?" Instead of saying never, and never would, whether or not they got into Harvard, Z sat there laughing in the sophisticated style of Mrs. R. and feeling compromised and phony and intimidated. Mr. R.'s Haydn got louder, more torn by anguish and humiliation.

§ Natural light passes through murky glass windows in the office doors and sinks into the brown linoleum floor. It is scuffed, heel-pocked, and burned where students ground out cigarettes while waiting to speak to their professors. The halls are long and wide, and have gloomy brown seriousness, dull grandeur. You hardly ever hear people laughing in them. The air is too heavy with significance. Behind the doors, professors are bent over student papers, writing in the margins B+, A−.

§ Henry comes to my office. "Free for lunch?" I jump up and say, "Give me a minute." He glances at his watch. I run to the men's room, start pissing, want to hurry. The door opens. It's Henry. Also wants to piss. He begins. I finish. Seconds go by and then a whole minute as he pisses with the force of a horse. He would have gone to lunch with me, carrying that pressure.

§ Boris asks my opinion of a certain movie that has been highly praised. I know it isn't any good, but I'm unwilling to say so. He'll ask why I think it isn't any good. I'd have to tell him, which would mean telling him about myself, becoming another object of endless, skeptical examination. I prefer to disappoint him immediately and not wait for the negative judgment, the disapproval and rejection, like one of his women who never know, from day to day, whether they are adored or despised. I confess, finally, that I disliked the movie, but I understand why many others loved it. The woman I live with has seen it several times. He laughs. He approves. I feel a rush of anxiety, as though I've said too much. I'll be haunted later by my remark, wondering what I told him inadvertently.

§ Boris had been very successful in Hollywood, but he didn't have one good thing to say about the industry or his colleagues. Producers were conniving, directors were bullies, stars were narcissistic imbeciles. Given his talent and brains, a little contempt for his colleagues was understandable, but he was bitter, he was seething. He went on and on, as if to prove that an emotion perpetuates itself, and then he told a story which I promised not to repeat, but I don't feel bound. Others heard him. He'd been invited to L.A. to meet a group of wealthy people who wanted him to write a movie on a loathsome subject. This was neither here nor there. Any subject, he said, can be made worthwhile. What matters is the way it's rendered. I disagreed, but he became impatient, he didn't want to discuss "art." He was too upset by life. He'd been offered for writing the movie a stupendous sum, endless cocaine, and a famous beautiful woman. When he said her name his voice leaped, spiraled up with revulsion, as if not to touch her. "They treated me like an animal."

"What did you say?"

"What do you think? I took the next plane home." Looking sullen, he said, "You think I'm a shmuck?"

§ Annette didn't want to go to Danny's. I followed her from room to room, cajoling, arguing. Not to go was not to live. It wasn't her idea of living. She didn't want to go, but she bought a few yards of silk and began to make herself a dress, working on it at night after the kids were in bed. None of her dresses was good enough. What about the dress she wore last week, the green dress, or what about the black dress? Anyhow, look, I've known Danny since we were kids. We played basketball together in the neighborhood. His mother knows my mother. It makes no difference that he's prospered and everyone at his party is likely to be rich except us.

Who'll care about your dress? It's a dinner party, not a
fashion show. More to the point, who will be as beautiful
as you?

I didn't say anything like that. She didn't want to go,
let alone talk about it. She was making a dress. That was
a sign. She hadn't actually said she was going, but why
else would she make a dress? So I phoned the babysitter. She didn't tell me not to phone the babysitter. Saturday came. She hadn't said she was going, but she moved
more slowly than usual. That was a sign. I didn't ask if
she was going. She might have felt challenged and said
no. She took much longer than usual with dinner for the
kids, much longer putting them to bed. I helped, but
nothing I did seemed to speed the process. She was
moving slowly, as if with weighty business on her mind.
I couldn't just say, "If we're going, let's move a little
quickly, all right?" The babysitter arrived, a cheery girl,
not too stupid. I read to the kids, then shut the lights
and said good night, and went to our room and saw that
she had put on the dress she made. Rose-colored silk.
Extremely simple sheath. I looked at her looking at
herself. She could tell what I felt, since there is every
sort of silence. My voice asked, "How does it feel to look
like you?" She said, "It's all right."

I imagined seeing myself like that. The surprise; the
little delirium. It must be frightening, pleasing. She'd
never admit she liked it. Me, I looked all right, but not
good enough for her. I wasn't rich enough either. If I
were rich, or an older man, we might connect better.

We'd have moral pathos; delicate binding sorrow. I said, "Are you ready?"

We drove to Danny's place, from flats to hills, from sycamores to Monterey pines. She didn't say a word, but she was in the car. She didn't have to talk. What did she owe the world? The evidence was in. Like a flower or a painting, her existence was enough. I wished she'd talk, just the same. I'd have been happier even if she complained, or if she were happier. But this was a lot. I didn't need more; except maybe a cigarette. She never objected to my smoking, but she was doing something for me. I could forgo.

There were twelve people at Danny's party. We knew some of them. Sooner or later, I'd slide up beside her and whisper, "What's that guy's name, the bald guy with the mustache?" She'd whisper it to me. She was talking to Danny's wife, doing fine, even if she was uncomfortable. She looked better than anyone in the room. Or California. Or the planet. I'd have whispered that to her, but she'd get annoyed, the way she got annoyed in bed. I had the wrong effect. I liked her too much. Always a mistake. You can't expect a woman to want you to like her too much.

The things I'd done in my frustration. I never dared think about that. I'd have denied it under torture. It wasn't a question of getting laid, only how. The ferocity. Could one live without it? Or with it? How was everyone living anyway? It was a secret. *The secret.*

She seemed to be having a good time. I always had a good time, being cruder stuff. Later in the car, still

———

high, I'd say something like "Well, didn't you have a good time?" She'd say, "No. Neither did anyone else." All the people laughing and talking, they'd been miserable. They didn't know it, but they'd had a truly lousy time. I'd want to scream and pummel the steering wheel, but I just drove more quickly. She'd say, "You'll hit a dog. Then you'll be sorry." I never hit anything, but I'd feel as if I hit a dog. It was lying in the street behind me, blood sliding from its mouth like an endless tongue. I was a good driver, fifty times better than she, but I slowed down. She slowed me down.

I was having a splendid time, drinking and eating like a king, feeling free to enjoy myself. A completely bullshit feeling, but it refused to be questioned. She seemed to be doing better than all right, sitting obliquely opposite me at the dinner table between a lawyer and a gay stockbroker, new friends of Danny's. I was his only old friend in the room. He wanted me to see his crowd, enjoy his new life. I was proud of him, happy for him. She turned to the lawyer, then to the stockbroker, whom I could see she preferred. No sexual tension. They could talk easily. She was a column of rose silk rising toward gray eyes. I'd have made a pass at her, the girl at the party, the one I was still dying to meet.

After coffee and dessert, somebody lit a marijuana. I was surprised, then figured it was the right touch. There was a Republican judge from San Diego at the table. A marijuana couldn't be more inappropriate, more licentious, but this was Berkeley. We were The People, fin-

———

ishing off a two-thousand-dollar dinner party with a joint. Danny knew how to make a statement.

The marijuana was moving around the table, everyone taking a drag, even the judge, consolidating our little community in crime. It would soon reach her. What would she do? She didn't even smoke. I tried not to stare, make her nervous. She took it with no sense of the thing in her fingers, as if it were a pencil, and tried to pass it straight on to the stockbroker. He urged her to take a drag. She looked from him to the lawyer. He, too, offered friendly encouragement. She lifted it to her lips and sipped a little, not to any effect, not really taking a drag. The ash was long and needed to be tapped off, or it might fall of its own, which it did. She jumped up, slapped at her lap. There was a black hole, the size of a penny, in the rose silk. The ash had burned through instantly, ruined her dress. Now the drive home, my speeding car, the bleeding dog.

§ That quick efficient feeling in the hands, plucking the shaft free of the pack, dashing a match head to perfection. Fat, seething fire. You pull the point of heat against tobacco leaf and a globe of gas rolls into the tongue's valley, like a personal planet. Then the consummation, the slithering hairy smoke. Its danger meets the danger we live with in the average street, our lethal food, poisoned air, imminent bomb. In Morocco and Berlin, in Honolulu's sunshine or the black Siberian night, in the cruel salons of urban literati, in the phantasmagoria of brothels, in rain forests full of orchids and wild pigs where women bleed to phases of the moon and men hunt what they eat, in the excremental reek of prison cells, or crouched beside a window with a gun in your lap, or sitting in your car studying a map, or listening to a lecture at the Sorbonne, or waiting for a bus or a phone call, or just trying to be reasonable, or staying up late, or after a meal in some classy restaurant, hands repeat their ceremony. The shock of fire. The pungent smoke. Disconnection slides across the yellowing eye. True, it's very like but morally superior to masturbation; and you look better, more dignified. We need this pleasing gas. Some of us can claim no possession the way a cigarette is claimed. What wonderful exclusiveness. In company a cigarette strikes the individual note. If it's also public suicide, it's yours. Or in the intenser moment after sexual disintegration, when the old regret, like a carrion bird, finds you naked, leaking into the night, a cigarette redeems the deep being, reintegrates a person's privacy. White wine goes with lobster. What goes with bad news so well as a cigarette? Imagine a common deprivation— say, a long spell of no sex—without a cigarette. Life isn't good enough for no cigarette. It doesn't make you god-like, only a little priest of fire and smoke. All those sensations yours, like mystical money. Such a shame they kill. With no regard for who it is.

§ Boris said that his first wife was a virgin. She came the first time they had sex. Worse, he says, she came every time after that. He watches my eyes to see if I understand why he had to divorce her.

§ The pain you inflict merely trying to get through the day. Pavese talks about this great problem. He had a woman in mind. Pavese does his work he kills her . . . Pavese reads a newspaper he kills her . . . Pavese makes an appointment to see an old friend . . . Finally, he killed himself. Sartre says to kill another is to kill yourself. He spent hours in coffee shops and bars. He liked to carry money in his pocket, lots of money. He compared it to his glasses and cigarette lighter. So many companions. He'd never have killed himself.

§ Self-pity is a corrupt version of honesty.

§ I tell Boris my grief. He says, "I know I'm supposed to have a human response, but I'm hungry."

§ Annette claimed Dr. Feller "worked hard" during their sessions. "I trusted him," she says. "So many therapists sleep with their patients." As if it were entirely up to him. That hurt my feelings. Later we met his girlfriend at a party. I was friendly, as usual, but Annette was furious, confused, depressed. I asked, "What's the matter?" She wouldn't answer, but then, in bed, unable to sleep, she announced, "I will confront him, tell him off." I ask, "Why?" She hisses, "I trusted him." I begin to wonder if I'm crazy. Dr. Feller took a fifth of my income. I feel a spasm of anger, but fall asleep anyway, imagining myself taking a three-point shot from the sideline with no time on the clock. The ball feels good as it leaves my hand.

§ I meet Eddie for lunch. He wants to talk, but is too agitated, doesn't know how to begin. We order this and that. He starts, tells me that his wife came to his office and made a scene. There were patients in the waiting room. He had to beg her to shut up till they got out in the street. It wasn't better in the street. She berated him, threatened to ruin his life. His eyes begin to glisten and now I can't eat. I imagine her yelling at him in front of his patients. I hear myself groan with sympathy. Then he says, "I bought a radio car. It's about this big." He raises his hands, holding them a foot and a half apart. "It's fast, too."

§ I was talking to Eddie about difficulties with my wife's lawyer. He cuts me off, very excited, nearly manic, shouting about difficulties with his wife's lawyer. "She snarls at me in legal letters, like I might forget this is war. I get very upset. I write back long angry letters. I tear them up, then write angrier letters and tear them up, too. Today I decided I can't write. I must phone and tell her what I think of her fucking letters. So I phoned. Soon as I say my name, her voice becomes high and warm. Like she is delighted to hear from me. I thought maybe I dialed the wrong number, reached her cunt. But you know what? I responded very warmly. Like a prick."

§ Women are tough. They know what they want. Men know more or less what they need, which is only what they like, not even what they need. King Lear wails, "But, for true need . . ." then can't define it. That's a real man.

§ My neighbor is building his patio, laying bricks meticulously. The sun beats on him. Heat rises off the bricks into his face. I'm in here writing. He'll have built a patio. I'll be punished.

§ X tells Y. Y repeats it to W and thus betrays X. The moment of telling, for X, felt like prayer, almost sanctified. He thinks the betrayal was evil, but evil lay in the telling, in daring to assume one could.

§ Spoke to her on the phone. She cried. Said she missed me. I feel like a ghoul wandering in this darkness.

§ The secretary said a long goodbye. A minuscule flake, like a fish scale, trembled in her right nostril. Her face shone with cosmetic oils, as in feverish sweating. I thought she loved me, and I was reluctant to meet her eyes. I could have kissed her, perhaps changed her life, made her a great pianist, or poet, or tennis star, kissing her every day.

§ Eddie says he wanted to run out into the street, grab the first person he saw, and tell that person everything. He wanted to tell everything to anybody. But he picked up the phone and dialed his girlfriend. When she said hello, the sweetness of her voice, which had always pleased him, enraged him. He spoke with strenuously deliberate slowness, as if to a very stupid person, as he told her about the burning sensation he felt that morning when he pissed. She made no comment, asked no question. She understood what he was getting at. With the same slowness, he continued to speak to her, now offering an analysis of her character, saying things she would never forget, frightening even to him when he thought later about what he'd said. She said, when he let her speak, "You didn't get it from me." He heard the pressure of feeling in her voice, and he knew that she wanted to say much more, but she could only manage to repeat, "You didn't get it from me." Then she hung up. Eddie phoned her again immediately, still angry but already regretful, and no less wretched, probably, than she. She wouldn't pick up the receiver. This struck him as unjust, but what could he do? He went into the next room. His wife, sitting at her desk, was writing a letter. She looked so much involved in her letter that Eddie was reluctant to say anything to her, but he couldn't be silent. The very sound of his voice, as he began, struck him as criminal, a violation of their peaceful domestic order. He was deeply ashamed as he said, "I have an infection." He was about to tell her about his girlfriend, but she thrust herself away from her desk, rushed toward him, sank to her knees, and clutched his legs. "I betrayed you," she said. "I betrayed you in every possible way." Eddie says it wasn't simply her confession that appalled him. It was the strangeness of her emotion and the way she begged, "Forgive me, forgive me." The words came from far away, like sounds in the night, as though he and she had nothing in common, only the darkness, and there couldn't even be anything to forgive.

─────

§ His neck was as thick as his head, and he had long heavy arms. His hands were stained black in the creases and in the cusp of his fingernails. Beside him stood a pale girl about nine years old. Too clean and pretty to be his daughter, but they had the same flat, grim expression and whenever he moved she moved. She was his daughter. They didn't talk to each other, didn't look at each other. He finished his business at the counter and turned to go. She turned to go. She walked step by step beside him out the door and into the parking lot. They looked sad. A brutalized man; a pale girl. As I watched them through the glass windows of the door, the man whirled suddenly, sweeping up the girl in his tremendous arms. She screamed. My heart bulged, as though I had to act quickly to save her, but her scream changed from terror to delight. My heart dissolved. That man would die for her. She hugged his monstrous neck. Would she find such love again?

§ Eddie invited his soon-to-be-former wife and her lover, a guy with two kids, over to his place for dinner. He cooked a duck, prepared a garden salad, and built a fire. They sat watching it after dinner, sipping cognac. His wife and her lover stayed the night. Eddie's house is big, lots of extra rooms. He says they talked for hours, but something was wrong. He keeps thinking about it. "I don't know," he says, "something was wrong." I laugh. He laughs, too, but I can tell he doesn't know what's funny.

§ I talk to Annette only on the phone. Afraid we might touch.

§ Henry is talking and eating a turkey sandwich. A piece of turkey falls out of his sandwich onto the floor. My life stops. What will he do? Something told me that he will go on talking as he picks it up and pops it into his mouth. He did exactly that. I felt we knew each other. At his funeral, I thought, I will cry.

§ I asked Boris to read my screenplay. Then I sat in his living room. He stood and spoke in complete sentences, built paragraphs, obliged me to read him. He wanted revenge for having done me a favor. I responded to him with laughter, dismay, surprise, assent, always appropriate and quick, feeling insulted by his concern for my edification. Other friends read it and said it isn't good; others said it is. One said, "The best screenplay in the world can be made into a lousy movie." Was the reverse also true? There was no truth.

§ Only desire and luck prevail in this world. If my screenplay isn't good, could it be bad enough to succeed?

§ Boris tells me he *really* loves Y and he REALLY wants to fuck X. Montaigne says there is more wildness in thinking than in lust.

§ Whatever was wrong was wrong from the instant we met, but like kids with big eyes we plunged into eating. Later she said, "I knew it instinctively. I could feel it was wrong." Even then she reached me, her voice speaking —beyond the words—of her. I must have the heart of a dog. I live beneath meaning.

§ I eat standing up, leaning over the sink.
I wouldn't eat like this if anyone could see me.

§ Her voice is flat and coolly distant, so I imagine things aren't over between us.

§ The distance between us is neither long nor short, merely imperishable, like the sentiment in an old song.

§ A huge fellow with the face of a powerful dullard stood behind the counter. He turned for items on the shelf and I saw that his pants had slipped below his hips, where he was chopped sheer from lower back to legs. No ass to hold up his pants. His bulk pushed forward and heaved up into his chest. He had a hanging mouth and little eyes with a birdlike shine. I bought salami and oranges from him.

§ Eddie said he ran into his former wife in the street in New York, and they talked. They talked as if neither of them knew how to say nice to see you, I'm expected somewhere, goodbye, goodbye. They went to a restaurant and ate and talked some more, and they went to her apartment, and they made love. Then she said, "So why did we get divorced?" Eddie smiled at me and said, "See?" as if he were the idiot of circumstances, shlepped into pain and confusion by his cock. "You know how long I was divorced before I remarried?" he asked. "Not three days," he said. I was sad for him and for her, and her, and her. The feeling widened like circles about a leaf fallen onto the surface of a pond.

§ We left Berkeley on December 14, driving south on Route 5, straight, flat road policed by aircraft. Jesse, eleven years old, twisted the radio dial searching for rock music. Ethan, fourteen, in the back seat with the luggage, was reading. For no reason, they'd begin to fight. Holding the wheel with one hand, I smacked at them with the other until they stopped. They were bored. There was nothing to see but the canal, a vein that leaked life out of Northern California into the agricultural empire of the Central Valley and beyond that into real estate from Los Angeles to Mexico.

At twilight we checked into a motel near Barstow. The boys chased each other about the room and began wrestling. I stepped outside and waited until they'd wrestled themselves into a stupor.

Early the next morning I woke them and said, "Shower and pack. We're going to the Grand Canyon. It's ten miles deep and full of snakes and panthers." They cheered. I left for the motel office. The sunlight was brassy, the air was cool. Big trucks running down the highway pulled at me. Get out in the energy. Go.

Behind the motel desk stood a woman about fifty, with a red loaf of hair, like body and blood mashed into her personal fashion statement. While figuring my bill she said, "Going home for the holidays?"

"I'm delivering my sons to their mother. We're divorced, passing them back and forth. I'm doing it for the first time." She looked up, startled. I was startled, too. I'd been babbling, as if I'd owed her a confession in exchange for what she offered in her hair. It got to me, bespeaking desire beyond consummation on this planet, bulging upward, packed and patted into shape, bursting with laborious and masturbatory satisfaction, like a bourgeois novel, the kind you live with for days or weeks, reading slowly, nourished by its erotic intimacies and the delicious anxieties of a plot, wishing it would never never end.

"I once drove my Labrador from Berkeley to Sacramento," I said, "and gave it to a family that could take care of it better than I could. Then I had to sit by the side of the road for half an hour, until I could stop crying and drive."

"You're talking about a dog?"

"Yes. A Labrador retriever. Now I'm going to New York."

"You're going a funny way to New York."

"We'll stop at the Grand Canyon and have some fun. I'm taking a southern route to avoid bad weather."

She stood very still, as my meaning sifted down and settled inside her like sediment in a wine bottle. I said again, "Bad weather." Her head dipped, the red dome a second head, making a slow double bludgeon of assent. "But it's better than none at all," she said.

"That's a fact."

"It is," she said. We smiled together. She was a nice lady. She had nice hair. I yearned to be within its fold. I yearned to be taken into her hair.

I returned to the room. The boys hadn't showered.

Their clothes were flung about everywhere. They sprawled on the beds, gleaming with violence that had ceased when they heard the key in the lock. Like my opponents in a rough game, evil half smiles on their faces, they waited for my move. I thought of strangling them, but nothing in me wanted to move. It was plain they didn't give a shit about the Grand Canyon.

§ At a place called Truck Stop, I ate lunch. Truckers lean toward each other, eating pills, coffee, and starch. They look fat, vibrant, seething with bad health.

§ Checked into a motel in Manhattan, Kansas, and got the last room. Though it was midnight, people were still arriving. The highway was loud throughout the night. American refugees seek the road, the road.

§ Infinitely clear sky and prairie of Kansas. I felt vulnerable, easily seen, as in the eye of God.

§ A farmer came into the diner. He wore a baseball cap with a long bill. He was very tanned and dusty, and moved ponderously with the pain of this long day. His hands were much bigger than the coffee cup in front of him. He stared at it. In his eyes, no ideas, just questions.

———

"What's this?" A coffee cup. "What do you do with it?" Pick it up. Between first and second question, no words. No words even in the questions.

§ A young couple sat opposite me. The woman was long and pale. Her husband not as tall as she. His double-breasted suit and dark shiny tie were very ugly. He'd tried to dress impressively, perhaps for an official occasion. She wore a hand-knit gray sweater, setting off her lovely pale complexion. She could have improved her husband's taste, but was maybe indifferent to it. He had thin, colorless hair and red-rimmed, obedient eyes. They flicked nervously in her direction, hoping for a command. He suggested a small-town bureaucrat whose every action is correct and never spontaneous, but he was in love with his wife and lived in agonizing confusion. He looked to her for sympathy. She offered none. She had what she wanted in life. It included this man, or such a man. She made him feel ashamed of himself, his needs.

§ New York. Mother's apartment. Moritz visits, tells a story. One freezing morning everybody had to go outside and watch a man be hanged. He'd tried to escape the previous night. Beside Moritz stood a boy, the man's brother. "His nose became red. It was so red," said Moritz. "That's what I remember." Moritz's eyes enlarge and his voice becomes urgent, as if it were happening again. His excitement isn't that of a storyteller. He can recite passages from *Manfred* in Polish, but he isn't literary. The experience is still too real to him. His memories are very dangerous. He fears another heart attack, but he tells about the camps. It should be remembered as he tells it. Freezing morning. The boy's red nose.

§ Alone, you hear yourself chewing and swallowing. You sound like an animal. With company everyone eats, talk obscures the noises in your head, and nobody looks at what your mouth is doing, or listens to it. In this high blindness and deafness lives freedom. Would I think so if I hadn't left her?

§ She screamed and broke objects. Nevertheless, I refused to kill her.

§ Jimmy phones me after midnight. He's been living in Paris. I haven't spoken to him for over a year, but I recognize his voice, and I recognize the bar, too, the only one in Berkeley Jimmy likes. I hear the din of a Friday night crowd and a TV. I imagine Jimmy standing in the phone booth, the folding door left open to let me know he doesn't want to make conversation. He says he needs five hundred and seventy dollars for his rent, which is due tomorrow. He wasted a month trying to find an apartment in Berkeley, and he'll lose it if he doesn't come up with five hundred and seventy dollars. He'll pay me back in a couple of days. I know he won't. He never pays me back. He says, "I would go to your place, but I'm hitting on some bitch. I just met her. I can't split." What about tomorrow morning? Impossible. "I don't know where I'll be," he says.

I get out of bed and put on my clothes. My hands tremble a little when I tie my shoelaces; I have to concentrate on the job like a kid who just learned how to do it. Then I drive across town to Brennan's, being careful to stop at stop signs. At night cops get lonely and need to have a word with you.

Brennan's is crowded and loud. I can't spot Jimmy, though he's the only black man in the room—if he's there. He is. He's waving to me from the bar. I must have been looking at him for a few seconds before I saw him, because he is laughing at me.

The woman on the stool beside him is wearing jeans and high heels. She's blond, like all his others. When I walk up, Jimmy turns his back to her, takes my hand. He doesn't introduce us. She looks away and begins watching the talk show on TV. I slip Jimmy the check I've written. He doesn't look at it as he folds it into his wallet and says, "Thanks, man. I'll pay you back. Have a drink." I tell him I'm not feeling good. I can't stay.

But he has ordered an Irish whiskey for me. It's waiting on the bar beside his own.

He tells the guy next to him there's a free stool at the end of the bar. Would he mind? The guy picks up his beer and leaves. I take his stool and Jimmy hugs me, laughing at this accomplishment. The blonde, on his other side, glances at me and then back to the TV as if she doesn't expect to be introduced and is indifferent, anyway. I wonder if the Irish whiskey will be good for my flu. My hand trembles when I pick it up. I ask Jimmy how it was in Paris. He says, "Oh, man, you know. I get tired of them, even the finest ones." The blonde, I suppose, is also fine. What lasts is him and me. This idea is at the margins of my mind, fever occupies the middle like a valley of fog. I know for sure Jimmy has flattering ways. He says, "Look, man, do you really want to do this?" He's studying my glazed eyes. I think he's concerned about my illness, and then realize he means the money. "Didn't I?" I say, reaching into my shirt pocket before I remember that I gave him the check. Now I'm embarrassed. "Talk about something else, will you?" I say, though he wants me to ease the burden of gratitude. I get out of bed with fever to give him money . . . I don't finish the thought. The blonde turns, looks at me with cold blue intelligent eyes, but I see better than she does. I see that the connection to Jimmy is her fate. He's going to hurt her. She holds her martini as if she is invincible, and smokes her cigarette in a world-weary manner. I say, "I'm sick, man. Would I be here if I didn't want to be?" The blonde half-laughs, more a cough than a laughing sound. She wants me to leave and shows it by putting down her martini and heading for the ladies' room. Jimmy turns and watches. Her jeans are cut for trouble. The door shuts behind her and Jimmy says, "Her name is Gunnel. She's bad."

He laughs, unable to contain his excitement. Then he slaps my arm, surprised by how entertaining I am, though I've been very dull. I laugh, too, but I won't ever give him another cent, I think. That's what I always think. Then one night the phone rings and he says, "Hey, man," his voice low and personal, like there's nobody in the world but him and me.

§ Boris drove past me in his new car, speeding down Euclid Avenue, picking his nose. He didn't see me. He was watching the road, driving fast, obsessed with his nose. Each life, says Ortega, is a perspective on reality.

§ Boris laughs at his unexpressed jokes, then gives me a compassionate look for having missed the point known only to himself.

§ I found a modest place with only three main dishes on the menu, none over ten bucks. Not good; not terrible.

Journal

In Oakland near the courthouse. Nobody I know is likely
to walk in. I don't remember the name of the place, I
never noticed. I was eating dinner and reading the legal
papers, telling myself they're written in English, they
will have a great effect on my life, so I should try to
understand them, I must be calm and read slowly, when
the door opens and lets in a draft with street noise and
perfume. The noise hits me like a personal criticism, the
perfume cuts through the steam coming off my plate. I
look toward the door. I see a white linen blouse, pearls,
and a face heavily made up, correct for the pearls but
not for dinner in this place. Maybe the pearls are to
suggest that she's meeting somebody here, but something tells me she is alone. Her green eye shadow is a
touch sloppy, as if she wants to be beautiful, but she has
troubles, agonies, who knows. Maybe she's a lawyer,
works too hard, and wishes she'd had a child instead of
a career. The green eye shadow, part of a mask, tells
more than it hides. I look away to avoid her feelings. I
don't know her. I'm eating dinner. I'll soon finish,
smoke a cigarette, and then go home to sleep without a
body against whose complications to press my own. The
food tastes like pork or chicken, but not enough like
either to create anxieties. I don't remember what I ordered, but it's boring. I like it.

I'm trying to eat and read, not to look at her, though
she is garishly depressed and sits five feet away. The
waiter goes to her. It's his job. She tells him she wants
the fish, but without sauce, and she would like it grilled,

not poached. I look. He starts to ask what else she wants. She interrupts, asks if the wine is dry. He says, "Yes." She says, "Very dry?" He says, "I'll ask," and hustles away to the kitchen. I hear him consult the chef in a foreign language, maybe Arabic. She calls from the table, "I don't want it if it isn't very dry." He comes back, whispers, "It's very dry." She then says that she'll have soup and salad, but no cream in the soup, and bring the salad dressing on the side, then adds "Please" with a too strong voice and a frightened stare, like a person who is basically shy, struggling to be forthright. Instead of forthright, a kind of begging enters her tone, almost sexual. She smiles, amused at having betrayed herself, and also as if the waiter must be grateful for such a gift, which has now established a bond between them. He smiles politely and hurries away, confused by messages. She sits alone. As the waiter goes about his business at other tables, a light inside her grows dim. She feels abandoned. I want to rise and go hug her, or at least mess up her clothes, but you can't do anything for anybody. "Oh, waiter," she cries, "could you please bring the bread now?" He starts for the bread. "And I'd like a little water." He hurries to her with bread and water, as if that's what she wants.

§ Every wildness plays with death. Washing your hands is a ritual to protect against death. The small correct things you do every day. Aren't there people who do nothing else? They have proper sentiments and beliefs. They are nice people. I wanted to do dull ordinary chores all day and be like nice people only to forget death, only to feel how I'm still alive.

§ The waiter does everything quick, everything right— no sauce on the fish, dry wine, salad dressing on the side. Then he bends over her and whispers, "Why are you angry?"

She says, "I'm not angry."

He says, "I can see that you're angry."

"I'm not angry."

"Didn't I bring you everything you asked for?" His voice becomes bigger, self-pitying. "Fish, soup, bread, wine. Everything you asked for."

She says, "I shouldn't have to ask."

The waiter walks away rolling his eyes. He doesn't understand American women. I rise, go to her table, and sit opposite her.

She says, "My name is Billy. What took you so long?"

§ She pressed my leg with hers under the table. Conversation stopped. She continued pressing, then pulled away abruptly. Conversation resumed. She did it to excite herself, that's all. Her makeup was sloppy, her clothes were stylish. She'd start to say something, then laugh and say, "No." I'd never seen anyone more depressed. She said, "Driving to work I brush my teeth. I'm the invisible woman."

I said, "I locked myself out of my office and my car. I don't even exist."

She said, "I lost my checkbook and sunglasses. Nobody needs them."

"I forgot my appointment. Nobody wants to meet me."

She frowned. "You're trying and that's sweet. But I don't care."

§ Billy says, "Why don't you let me do it? Afraid you might like it?"

§ Billy phones, says, "Want to play?" I think about it, then say, "The traffic is heavy. It will take forever to get to your place. I can't stay long. I'd feel I'm using you. It's not right. I don't want to use you." She says, "But I want to be used." I drive to Billy's place. She opens the door naked, on her knees. We fuck. "Do you think I'm sick?" she says. I say, "No." "Good," she says, "I don't think you're sick either."

§ You know your feelings, so you mistrust them, as if they belonged to an unreliable stranger. He behaved badly in the past and is likely to do so again. But you can't believe that. You believe you've changed. Then it happens again and the same feelings surprise you. Now you're fearful of yourself.

§ If there are things I'd never tell a psychotherapist, I would waste time and money talking to one. It would feel like a lie. I need a priest.

§ Sex in one place. Feeling in another.

§ Afterwards, afterwards, it is more desolating than when a good movie ends or you finish a marvelous book. We should say "going," not "coming." Anyhow, the man should say, "Oh, God, I'm going, I'm going."

§ Schiller says, "When the soul speaks, then—alas—it is no longer the soul that speaks." William Blake says, "Never seek to tell thy love / Love that never told can be." They mean the same as Miles Davis's version of "My Funny Valentine," so slowly played, excruciating, broken, tortured.

§ She wore baggy pants, a man's sweater, no makeup, and had strong opinions about everything, as if to show, despite her exceedingly beautiful face and body, she damn well had a mind. I felt sick with regret at having met her, ready to forgive every fault, half in love with a woman I won't ever see again.

§ The soul is known through intuitions, or forms without meaning—like fish, flowers, music . . . Certainly not a face.

§ "Do you think it's possible to have fifteen sincere relationships?"

"Not even one," says Billy. "Let me tie you to the bed."

"No."

"Why not?"

"Because I don't want you to."

"I'll stop when you tell me. Just don't say 'stop.' That only excites me. Say 'tomato' or something."

§ Deborah wants to have her eyes fixed so they'll look like white eyes and she hates her landlady who gave her the Etna Street apartment, choosing her over 157 other applicants. Her landlady assumed Deborah is a good girl, clean and quiet. "A Japanese angel," says Deborah with a sneer. I was shocked by her racism. I hadn't imagined that she thought of herself as Japanese. She showed me photos of her family. Mother, father, brothers, sister—all Japanese, but I hadn't supposed she thought she was, too. What the hell did I imagine? Never to have to think of yourself as white is a luxury that makes you deeply stupid.

§ Deborah holds a new blouse up to her chin, tilts her head, and says, "Do you like this blouse?" I look at it and at her, how she's tilted her head so seriously, waiting for my opinion, but I can't speak. She sees what's happening and lowers the blouse. Her head remains tilted like an iris on the fine white stalk of her neck. She whispers, as if there were someone else in the room, "You're hopeless. You're like my girlfriend. I ask if she likes what I'm wearing and she says, 'You're beautiful.' "

§ Margaret says she went to Cesar's Latin Palace and stood at the bar until some guy asked her to dance, a handsome Jamaican. Great dancer. She says there's a divorced couple at Cesar's who will not have anything to do with each other, except they show up Saturday night and they dance together, drawn to the music in each other's body. When the number ends they separate instantly, without a word, and go to different tables. They'd rather drink with strangers. Then the great Francisco Aquabella starts slapping conga drums, driving the whole world to cha cha cha, and she feels the need for him, that one, the guy over there across the floor sitting with the white bitch, that one who is standing up and crossing the floor to her table, and she is standing up, too, even before he asks her to dance, feeling the music in his body. Don't talk to me about love. Talk about cha cha cha, and the way he touches her. His eyes are cold, yet full of approval. When they dance, they belong to each other and nothing else matters until the music ends.

§ Kittredge loves pretty women, but he is blind, can't pursue them. So I take him to a party and describe a woman in the room. He whispers, "Tell me about her neck." Eventually I introduce him to her. They leave the party together. Kittredge is always successful. Women think he listens differently from other men. In his blind hands they think pleasure is truth. Blind hands know deep particulars, what yearns in neck and knee. Women imagine themselves embracing Kittredge the way sunlight takes a tree. He says, "Talk about her hips." As I talk, his eyes slide with meanings, like eyes in a normal face except quicker, a snapping in them. Kittredge cannot see, cannot know if a woman is pretty. I say, "She has thick black hair." When they leave together I begin to sink. I envy the magnetic darkness of my friend. To envy him without desiring his condition is possible.

§ Evelyn told me that Sally, her dearest friend—"Don't ever repeat this!"—came down with the worst case of herpes the doctor had ever seen.

§ Evelyn's four-year-old son had a nightmare in which Evelyn appeared with a big knife stuck in her head. She has scheduled him for psychotherapy five days a week.

§ Margaret says she went back to Cesar's. The Jamaican asked her to dance again. She refused. She liked him, but she kept a closed face. If she showed interest, he'd think she was in the same mood as last time. They would dance, then go out to his car and make love. She said, "I have a Ph.D. I can do anything. I can even read fashion magazines. He's a nice guy, but he'd never understand me."

§ Deborah's dentist, a little Jewish man, talks incessantly and she can't say a word because her mouth is under investigation by steel instruments and also hooked like a fish by a suction tube. Nevertheless, her dentist says things that require an answer, so she grunts and moans to say yes, no, really, how nice, too bad. Last time she saw him he carried on about Buddhism, which he studies with monks in a temple. He said, incidentally, that he'd learned to levitate. When he finished working, Deborah could talk. She asked if he meant "meditate" rather than "levitate." He said, "No. I meant levitate." She asked him to show her. He said, "No, no." She pleaded with him. He refused. She refused to leave. He said, "Just once." He turned his back to her, crouched slightly, and lifted off the floor. I waited for Deborah to continue, but that was the end. She had no more to say. I snapped at her, "He did not levitate." She said, truly astonished, "He didn't?"

§ Evelyn goes shopping Monday through Sunday. Clothes, jewelry, books, records, prints, paintings, ceramics. Her house of many things shrieks good taste. The latest dress style isn't always right for Evelyn, but she is the first in town to wear it. She believes her clothing and her automobile say something about her. After shopping, Evelyn feels she's done good. She must know she is too wide for a zebra-striped dress, but still, it's the most new thing, and it gives her moral sensations to wear it with bright red socks, her black pearl necklace, and a wide aluminum belt. All of it is hidden under her black cape, which she throws off in the restaurant, driving the women in the place mad with envy.

§ Margaret doesn't like oral sex because she was once forced to do it at gunpoint, in a car, in the parking lot next to the railroad tracks, outside the bar where the guy picked her up. I wish she hadn't told me. I hear freight trains. I see people coming out of the bar, laughing, drunk, going to their cars while she crouches in misery and fear, the gun at her head. How easy, if I had the gun at his head, to pull the trigger.

§ Eddie calls her Stop-and-Go. She's up early and moving, then collapses into hours of marijuana. It's like everything with her, he says. No degrees. Truth or lies, good or bad, stop or go. She criticizes Eddie constantly. He can't do anything right. He wants to break up, but plans to provoke her into doing it by hanging a picture she doesn't like in a place she finds disturbing. She'll see that he is saying the house is his. She'll go. He says she becomes affectionate after a fight. He finds her adorable then. He says she dislikes his father for his Jewish traits, and also dislikes Eddie for his. He says she doesn't even know what they are, then smiles in a silly way, as if he weren't really offended. Tomorrow her mood will be different. She'll forget what she said today. Her feelings aren't moored to anything, no important work, like his medical practice, for example. He is accomplished; successful. The woman is merely herself, except when she objects to him. He thinks it costs him nothing and it makes her feel real. He says, "Let me ask you something. You and me, we've had dinner together a couple of hundred times. Is there anything about how I eat that looks to you Jewish?"

"Is that what she thinks?"

"How I eat, how I dress, how I talk, how I fuck."

I laugh.

"Okay. She doesn't treat me well," he says. "She disapproves of me. Criticism is my daily bread. But I'm never lonely with her, never bored. I'm miserable. But this word 'miserable,' in my case, is not the end of the discussion. It's only the beginning. There are kinds of misery . . ."

Feelings swarm in Eddie's face, innumerable nameless nuances, like lights on the ocean beneath a sky of racing clouds. Eddie could have been a novelist or a poet. He has emotional abundance, fluency of self. He's shameless.

"Believe me, I'm not a faithful type. I've slept with a hundred other women. More. But it's no use. She hits me, curses me. She says, 'I don't want to be touched. I don't want to be turned on.' No matter. It begins to happen. She relaxes, lets me disgrace myself. She tells me how. 'Lick the insides of my legs while I make this phone call.' My father slaved six days a week, year after year, to put me through medical school. For this he went to an early grave."

§ The paper was thick and creamy, textured like baby flesh. Every night she opened to a new page, wrote the date, then "Dear Diary," then thought for a minute, then quit. After a while it came to her that she had no internal life. Ortega says this is true of monkeys. But monkeys are known to dream. Evelyn says, "I never had a dream."

§ She was once making love and the bed collapsed on her cat, who was asleep underneath, and broke its back. Since then, Margaret says, sex hasn't been the same for her. Then she dashes to the sink, grabs a knife, and looks back at me, her teeth shining, chilly as the steel, welcoming me to the wilderness.

§ Margaret tells me her lover is wonderful. "He makes me feel like a woman," she says, "without degrading me." I don't know what she means, but can't ask. What is it to feel like a woman? or to be made to feel that way?

§ I said to Margaret, "When we talk we make a small world of trust." Quickly she says, "There are men so loose of soul they talk even in their sleep." She laughs, surprised by her good memory and how wonderful Shakespeare is. She didn't get it right, but it no longer mattered what I was going to say.

§ I asked Deborah out to dinner. She said, "You looking for an exotic date or something?" Now she tells me that she went to an orgy in Berkeley. It was highly organized.

On Wednesday, everyone met at the home of the couple, an engineer and his wife, who organized it. People talked, got to know one another, then went home. They returned on Friday and took off their clothes. "You didn't have to undress or do anything," said Deborah. "I only wanted to watch." But so many of them begged her to undress that she finally consented, except for her underwear. Then she lay on the floor. The engineer, his wife, and their friends, all of them naked, kneeling on either side of her, mauled her. She was being polite.

"A Japanese angel."

"I didn't behave like them," she said.

§ Sonny was my best friend. Then she says, "I met a man last night." My heart grew heavy. I couldn't count on her anymore for dinner, long talks on the telephone, serious attention to my problems, and she'd no longer tell me about herself, how well or ill she slept last night, and whether she dreamed, and what she did yesterday, and what people told her and she them. She said, "I don't know why, but I feel guilty toward you."

I said, "What's he like?" She said he is some kind of a psychotherapist, divorced, lives in Mill Valley. His former wife is Korean, a fashion model. She made him install a plate-glass window in their living room so birds would fly into it and break their necks. She had them stuffed.

"Oh, I know the guy," I said. "Women find him attractive."

"How do men find him?"

I was conscious of the danger.

"He dresses well. He likes classical music and hiking. He goes sailing. He's a good cook. Doesn't smoke."

"You think he's a prick."

§ Sonny was six years old when she went up on a roof with a boy. He pulled down his pants. She pulled down hers. They looked. Years later she still worried about what she'd done, thinking she could never be famous because the boy would tell everybody she'd pulled her pants down. She was a success in school and had innumerable boyfriends. None of that changed anything for her. At the age of six, in a thoughtless moment, she ruined her life.

§ Billy comes to my office, sits, looks me in the eye, and says, "Girls like to be spanked."

§ Sonny will see the man, sleep with him, then linger in regret to the end. If I said, "I know for certain he has leprosy," she would still see the man, etc. Nobody passes up romance.

§ Sonny says she dislikes being touched by doctors. I thought to remind her, but she said quickly, "He's different." With me—as if talking to herself—she needn't bother about little connections.

§ There was a message for me at the motel. I hoped it was Sonny, but it's from Evelyn. "Call immediately." I call. The crazy pitch of her hello means she bought something or she met a famous person. I'm wrong. She says, "I went to a garage sale in the Oakland hills. Are you listening? There was a Swedish dresser with glass pulls. Inside one drawer I see a piece of paper, like folded in half. I opened it. It's a sketch in red crayon. Old, but nice, not faded. I scrunched it quick into my purse. I also got a pewter dish and a pocket watch. I went home. No, first I met Sheila for coffee. I didn't tell her what I got. She's so jealous. Later I went home and took the sketch out of my purse. I smoothed it out. It's the head of a woman, signed by Raphael. I almost died. So I phoned Sheila—"

"You stole a Raphael?"

"Listen, I almost died. Sheila has a friend in the art department at Berkeley. I called him and went to his office. He almost died. He said it looks authentic, but he couldn't be positive. He told me to mail it to a man in England. The greatest living expert. So I mailed it to him."

"Insured?"

"Regular mail. Listen. Listen, the expert just phoned me. He says he almost died. It's authentic. But listen. Wait till you hear what else . . ."

§ Sonny tells me she will separate her emotional life from her sexual feelings. "In other words," she said, "I'll have an affair only if I can't become entangled with the man."

"In other words, you're already doing it."

"How embarrassing . . . I lied."

§ Byron says, "And, after all, what is a lie? 'Tis but the truth in masquerade."

§ Are some truths told by lying?

§ Eddie met the woman years ago, in another state, prior to her divorce, long before she changed her hairstyle and became a different person. His own hair, though beginning to gray, was much the same. He figures she recognized him immediately, but since he didn't recognize her, she didn't tell him they'd met before. Both acted as if neither were part of the other's past, even after they'd slept together again. Eddie imitated himself: "Oh, did you grow up in Michigan?" By then he knew she had.

He remembered. Years earlier, he now remembered, the first time they made love, he'd asked, "How do you handle your feelings?" She had told him, in the tender darkness, that she loved her husband.

"Why are you doing this with me?"

"This is this," she said, "and that is that."

It would have been possible early on, with only a little embarrassment, to stop pretending.

"Don't you remember me?"

"Should I? Wait, oh no. Oh no. This can't be happening. You're not Eddie Finger, are you?"

But Eddie didn't, or couldn't, stop pretending. Naturally, then, she couldn't either. He told himself that she didn't want to be recognized. Why else would she have changed her look? She actually did look different. Time passed. Then it was too late. It was impossible to stop pretending. Too much was invested in the lie, the black hole of their romance into which everything sucked. He thinks she knew he knew she knew he knew. He couldn't go on with it. There was too much not to say. He stopped seeing her. "She waits for me in hell," he says. "We'll discuss it then. But she'll have changed her hair, you know what I mean?"

§ Breakfast with Henry near campus. A strange woman joined us at the table. She smoked my cigarettes and took my change for her coffee. In her purse she had a fold of bills compressed by a hair clip. "My tuition fee," she said. Henry smiled and carried on as if she weren't there. He said one of his colleagues felt happy when he turned fifty because he no longer desired the pretty coeds. He would concentrate on biochemistry, get a lot of work done, not waste time fucking his brains out. Henry laughed. He didn't believe in this lust for biochemistry. The woman, pretending to study for a German class, looked up from her grammar and said, "I will learn every word."

§ It was cold, windy, beginning to rain. Deborah was afraid she wouldn't find a taxi. She'd have to walk for blocks in the rain. She didn't want to go, but her psychotherapist wasn't charging her anything. A few months back, she told him she couldn't afford to continue. He lowered the rate to half. Even that became too much for her, so he lowered it to nothing. She stood, collected her things, and pulled on her coat like a kid taking orders from her mother, then fussed with her purse, her scarf, trying to be efficient but making dozens of extra little moves, rebuttoning, untying and retying her scarf, and then reopening her purse to be sure there was enough money for a taxi if she could find one. She wanted to stay, talk some more, but couldn't not go to her psychotherapist. She felt he really needed her.

§ Sonny says, "The woman can't understand any experience not her own. She's Irish." She didn't mean because she's Irish. She meant thin, practical, cold. She meant not like herself, dark and warm. She meant blond. In effect, the way people talk is what they mean. It is precise and clear—more than mathematics, legal language, or philosophy—and it is not only what they mean, but also all they mean. That's what it means to mean. Everything else is alienation, except poetry.

§ Sonny has green eyes. I can't not see them.

§ Sonny's teeth are crooked. I can't not desire to lick them.

§ I think of Sonny's terrible flaws. I love her flaws.

§ I'm so furious at Sonny I almost hate her.

§ I told Sonny I love her. She said, "I'm a sucker for love."

§ Sonny strides toward me across the room holding something behind her back. Her face is expressionless. Then she raises her hand above her head and I see she is holding her high-heeled shoe. She brings it down, trying to spike the top of my head, but I grab her wrist, wrench her about, shove her away. She falls into the chair and sits as she fell, arms limp, legs sprawled apart. I go to her, drop to my knees, and hug her about the waist. She says, "Intimacy brings out the worst in us," and then whispers, "I want to pull your whole head into my cunt."

§ We made love all afternoon. Sonny said, "Was it good?" My speech was slurred: "Never in my life . . ." She said, "I should be compensated."

§ Sonny reads in the paper about a child who was sexually assaulted and murdered. She says quietly, as if to herself, "What are we going to do about sex?"

§ We made love all afternoon. Sonny asked, "Was it good?" I said, "Never in my life," etc. The irrelevance of words, the happiness of being free of all such clothing. I lie on my back. Dumb. Savoring dumbness. My mother said she found my father on his back on the bedroom floor, staring up at her with a dumb little smile on his face, as if it weren't bad being dead. He'd gone like himself, a sweet gentleman with fine nervous hands, not wanting her to feel distressed. It's a mystery how one learns to speak, the great achievement of a life. But when the soul speaks—alas—it is no longer the soul that speaks.

§ There used to be desert. Now there are banks, office buildings, shopping malls, and wide roads striking in all directions, rolling with cars—going away, going away—pressed by unresisting emptiness. Nothing says stay. Nothing speaks to you, except the statue of John Wayne. I waited there, in front of the terminal building, studying him. (Sonny was late.) Nine feet tall, cast in brownish metal, he wears a cowboy outfit—wide-brimmed hat, gun belt, boots, spurs. The big body, a smidgeon too big for the head, goes lumbering toward the traffic. Beneath his hat is the familiar sunlight-cutting squint and tight dry scowl. He sees no traffic, no concrete or asphalt. He sees the California desert of long ago, the desert of his mind. No woman was ever late for "Duke."

The afternoon sky was purest blue, without birds or clouds. It was perfect until planes appeared, flickering specks. I'd hear their engines as they descended. It seemed I'd heard dozens of them. I stopped looking at my watch, stopped waiting for her.

Light sank into bluer and bluer blue. Air moved in

swift, thin currents, like ghostly fibers drawn across my cheeks. John Wayne's metal face had an underwater glare; eel-like menace. Cars pulled up. Travelers hurried to night flights. She'd been happy to hear from me. "Are you in town?" she cried. Her enthusiasm must have leaked away when she hung up the phone. Maybe she'd checked the mirror and seen something to discourage her; or she'd had an accident driving to the airport. I wasn't thinking about her when the apparition appeared. "I've been looking at you," it said, "standing right here looking at you." Sonny's hair, freshly washed and brushed, released airy strands of light. She shook her head, as if to deny what she couldn't help believing.

"You're very late," I said.

"You can beat me."

"My plane leaves soon."

"Miss your plane."

I already knew I would.

"I didn't just come straight from my office," she said. "I had to go home first, shower and dress. Look, I'm here. Aren't you a little happy to see me?" She took my arm, squeezing it as she pressed against my side, saying, "I'm hungry," walking me away toward her car.

We ate in a restaurant near the ocean, then went to a bar. An old black man, wearing glasses, played sentimental songs on the piano.

Sonny said, her hand stroking mine, "Nothing is going to happen. I don't care how sad you look."

"I missed you."

"We never got along." She took a cigarette from my pack and shoved the matchbook toward me.

"I think about you every day."

"What do you think?"

"What do you suppose?"

"Nothing is going to happen."

Strolling in the balmy night, we stopped and kissed, holding each other long after the urge subsided. The ocean raved in darkness.

"Don't feel me," she said.

"You feel good."

"Men don't turn. I go by and that's all."

"Does it matter?"

"They used to say, 'Wow.' 'Mamma mia.' Of course it matters. It's a way of being."

"It's savage."

"Nothing else is real."

I heard the dull repeated crash along the beach. I smelled the ocean's salt on Sonny's skin.

She stood at the bathroom mirror, making up her face. Tiny jars of cosmetics clanked against the sink, like stray notes of a wind chime. I sat on the edge of the tub.

"I hadn't planned to stay," I said.

She didn't answer at first. She unbuttoned her dress, letting the top fall about her hips, not to be soiled by makeup. She wore no bra. Leaning close to the mirror, she did her eyes, restoring shadows with brush and fingertip. I watched her rebuilding her look, perfecting it. She drew back, studying her work as she said, "I don't know why you phoned. Anyhow, I don't care."

"Must you say that?"

"Sad, isn't it? I used to get excited looking at you. But all you ever wanted was to fuck me. Admit it. Come on, be honest." She leaned toward the mirror again, speaking to herself. "It's hard work being beautiful. See this line?"

"What line?"

"This line. It wasn't there last week."

In a minute, she'd be out the door, gone. I imagined the empty motel room. I stood, pressed against her back, my cheek against hers in the mirror. I held her breasts. Her mirrored eyes remained blind to me. She said, "I knew you'd do that."

"I'll stay another day."

Her blind eyes widened, as if to see what I meant.

"I don't want to make you stay. You have your job, your family." Her tone was principled. She tugged up the top of her dress, buttoned it.

"It's what I want."

"I don't want you to do anything you don't want to do."

"We'll sleep late, then go someplace."

"Have a cigarette. We'll talk. You never really talked to me. Then I'll get out of here."

I held her hand, leading her from the mirror. She sat on the edge of the bed, her legs crossed, and watched me with no expression as I kneeled. I took off her shoes. She let me take off her dress—"No, don't . . ."—slowly.

Her voice was the slithery, labile silk sliding away as she lay back, eyes shut, hands resting on the pillow.

Ocean made its word.

Far far away, John Wayne endured the blaze of traffic.

"Talk," she whispered.

"About what?"

"Why did you phone me?"

"Why did you meet me?"

"What if I didn't love you anymore?"

"I'd die."

"I've been with a man. Are you dying?"

"Tell me."

"He was so handsome he scared me. Do you want to hear?"

"Yes."

"Does it turn you on?"

"I love your pleasure."

"Hold me," she whispered, then slept, her body fused along my side, breathing as I breathed.

Ocean fell along the beach.

I heard the god of night heaving a great sheet and hauling it back, and then heaving it again, trying to make his bed.

My Father

§ Six days a week he rose early, dressed, ate breakfast alone, put on his hat, and walked to his barbershop at 207 Henry Street on the Lower East Side of Manhattan, about half a mile from our apartment. He returned after dark. The family ate dinner together on Sundays and Jewish holidays. Mainly he ate alone. I don't remember him staying home from work because of illness or bad weather. He took few vacations. Once we spent a week in Miami and he tried to enjoy himself, wading into the ocean, being brave, stepping inch by inch into the warm blue unpredictable immensity. Then he slipped. In water no higher than his *pupik*, he came up thrashing, struggling back up the beach on skinny white legs. "I nearly drowned," he said, very exhilarated. He never went into the water again. He preferred his barbershop to the natural world, retiring, after thirty-five years, only when his hands trembled too much for scissors and razors, and angina made it impossible for him to stand for hours at a time. Then he took walks in the neighborhood, carrying a vial of whiskey in his shirt pocket. When pain stopped him in the street, he'd stand very still and sip his whiskey. A few times I stood beside him, as still as he, waiting for the pain to end, both of us speechless and frightened.

He was vice-president of his synagogue, keeping records, attending to the maintenance of the building. He spoke Yiddish, Polish, maybe some Russian, and had the Hebrew necessary for prayers. He spoke to me in Yiddish until, at about the age of six, I began speaking to him mainly in English. When he switched from one language to the other, I'd rarely notice. He could play the violin and mandolin. As a youth in Poland, he'd been in a band. When old friends visited our apartment, he'd drink a *shnaps* with them. He smoked cigars and pipes. He read the Yiddish newspaper, the *Forward*, and the *Daily News*. He voted Democratic but had no faith in politicians, political systems, or "the people." Aside from family, work, and synagogue, his passion was friends. My mother reminded me, when I behaved badly, of his friends. She'd say, "Nobody will like you." Everybody liked Leon Michaels.

He was slightly more than five feet tall. My mother is barely five feet. Because I'm five nine, she thinks I'm a giant. My father came from Drohiczyn (Dro-hee-chin), a town on the river Bug near the Russian border. When

My Father

I visited Poland in 1979, I asked my hosts about Drohiczyn. They said, "You'll see new buildings and Russian troops. No reason to go there." I didn't go there. It would have been a sentimental experience, essentially empty. My father never talked about the town, rarely said anything about his past. We also never had deep talks of the father-and-son kind, but when I was fifteen I fell in love and he said a memorable thing to me.

The girl had many qualities—tall, blond, talented musician—but mainly she wasn't Jewish. My father learned about her when we were seen together watching a basketball game at Madison Square Garden, among eighteen thousand people. I'd been foolish to suppose I could go to the Garden with a blonde and not be spotted. My father had many friends. You saw them in his barbershop, "the boys," snazzy dressers jingling coins in their pockets or poor Jews from the neighborhood who came just to sit, to rest in their passage between miseries. Always a crowd in the barbershop—cabdrivers, bookies, waiters, salesmen. One of them spotted me and phoned my father. When I returned that night, he was waiting up with the fact. He said we would discuss it in the morning.

I lay awake in anguish. No way to deny the girl I loved. I'd been seeing her secretly for months. Her parents knew about the secrecy. I was so ashamed of it that when I called for her I'd ring the bell and then wait in the street. She urged me to come upstairs, meet her parents. After a while, I did. They understood. Her previous boyfriend was the son of a rabbi.

In the morning my father said, "Let's take a walk." We walked around the block, then around the block again, in silence. It took a long time, but the silence was so dense it felt like one infinitely heavy immobilized minute. Then, as if he'd rehearsed a speech and dismissed it, he sighed. "I'll dance at your wedding."

Thus we spent a minute together, father and son, and he said a memorable thing. It is concise, its burden huge. If witty, it's in the manner of Hieronymus Bosch, making a picture of demonic gaiety. My wedding takes place in the middle of the night. My father is a small figure among dancing Jews, frenzied with joy.

For a fifteen-year-old in love, this sentence was a judgment, punishment, and release from brutal sanctions. He didn't order me not to see her. I could do as I pleased. As it happened, she met someone else and broke up with me. I was very hurt. I was also relieved. My father danced at my wedding, twelve years later, when I married Sylvia. Black-haired. Dark-skinned. Jew. Because her parents were dead, the ceremony was held in our apartment. Her aunts and uncles sat along one wall, mine along another. The living room was small. Conversation, forced by closeness, was lively and nervous. The rabbi, delayed by traffic, arrived late, and the ceremony was hurried. Everyone seemed to shout instructions. Did she circle me or I her? My father was delighted. When Sylvia and I fought, which was every day, she'd sometimes threaten to tell my father the truth about me. "It will kill him," she said.

I'd tried once to talk to him about our trouble. He wouldn't hear it. "She's an orphan. You cannot abandon her."

If he ever hit me, I don't remember it, but I remember being malicious. My brother, three years younger than I, was practicing scales on my father's violin. When he finished, he started to carry the violin across the room. I put out my foot. He tripped, fell. We heard the violin hit the floor and crack. Quicker than instantly, I wanted to undo the act, not trip my brother. But it was done. I was stuck with myself. I think I smiled. My father looked at the violin and said, "I had it over twenty years."

Maybe I tripped my brother because I'm tone-deaf. I can't learn to play a musical instrument. Nothing forgives me. I wish my father had become enraged, knocked off my head, so I could forget the incident. I never felt insufficiently loved, and yet I think: When Abraham raised the knife to Isaac, the kid had it good.

In photos, however badly lit or ill-focused, my father looks like himself. I never look like myself. This isn't me, I think. Like a baby, my father is inevitably himself.

My father never owned a car or flew in an airplane. He imagined no alternatives to being himself. He had his family, his friends, his neighborhood, synagogue, and the hectic variety of human traffic in the barbershop and the streets. Looking out my window above San Francisco Bay, I think how my father saw only Monroe Street, Madison Street, and Clinton Street. For thirty-five years, he walked to work.

I was in London, returning from three months in Paris, when he died. My flight to New York had been canceled. I was stranded, waiting for another flight. Nobody in New York knew where I was. I couldn't be phoned. The day after the funeral, I arrived. My brother met me at the door of the apartment and told me the news. I went alone to my parents' bedroom and sat on the bed. I didn't want to be seen crying.

A great number of people visited the apartment to offer condolences and to reminisce. Then a rabbi came, a tiny, fragile man dressed in black, with a white beard twice the length of his face. It looked like the top of his shirt. He asked my mother to give him some of my father's clothes, particularly things he'd worn next to his skin, because he was a good man, very rare. As the rabbi started to leave with a bundle of clothes in his arms, he noticed me sitting at the kitchen table. He said in Yiddish, "Sit lower."

I didn't know what he was getting at. Did he want me to crouch? I was somehow susceptible to criticism.

My mother interceded. "He feels," she said. "He feels plenty."

"I didn't ask how he feels. Tell him to sit lower."

I got up and left the kitchen, looking for a lower place to sit. I was very angry but not enough to start yelling at a fanatical midget. Besides, he was correct.

One Friday night, I was walking to the subway on Madison Street. My winter coat was open, flying with my stride. I wore a white shirt and a sharp red tie. I'd combed my hair in the style of the day, a glorious pompadour fixed and sealed with Vaseline. I was nineteen-years-old-terrific. The night was cold, but I was hot. The wind was strong. My hair was stronger. It gleamed like black, polished rock. As I entered the darkness below the Manhattan Bridge, where it strikes across Madison Street and makes a high, gloomy, mysterious vault, I met my father. He was returning from the barbershop, following his usual route. His coat was buttoned to the chin, his hat pulled down to protect his eyes. He stopped. As I approached, I saw him study me, his creation. We stood for a moment beneath the bridge, facing each other in the darkness and wind. An American giant, five feet nine inches tall. A short Polish Jew. He said, "Button your coat. Everybody doesn't have to see your tie."

I buttoned my coat.

"Why don't you wear a hat?"

I sighed. "I'm all right."

"You need a haircut. You look like a bum."

"I'll come to the barbershop tomorrow."

He nodded, as if to say "Good night" and "What's the use." He was on his way home to dinner, to sleep. He'd worked all day. I was on my way to sexual adventure. Then he asked, "Do you need money?"

"No."

"Here," he said, pulling coins from his coat pocket. "For the subway. Take."

He gave.

I took.

To Feel These Things

§ My mother, Anna Czeskies, was seventeen when she married and said goodbye to her parents in Brest Litovsk. She sailed to New York, settled in Coney Island, and moved later to a tenement in Manhattan, near my father's barbershop. Soon afterwards, the year Hitler came to power and Roosevelt was elected President, I was born. These names, intoned throughout my childhood, belonged to mythical deities. One was evil. The other was the other.

My mother's family intended to follow her to America, but the day my grandfather went to get their emigration papers there was a pogrom. He was attacked in the street by a mob and left for dead. He didn't recover quickly. Then it was too late to get out of Poland.

In photos he is pale and thin. Skin pulls tight across sharp bones in a narrow face. He has the alert, hypersensitive look of an ill-nourished person, but sits correctly, posing in the old style, as if a photo is serious business. He was a tailor who made uniforms for Polish army officers and had a feeling for posture. My mother says they threw his unconscious body into a cellar. I heard the story around the time children hear fairy tales. Once upon a time my grandfather was walking in the street . . .

Years later I would hear that organized terrorism had been reported for centuries in Europe, Russia, and the Middle East. Rabbinical commentaries engaged questions as to whether the community should surrender a few to save the rest, die with the few, or resist. Rabbis consulted the commentaries while the SS prepared gas chambers and worked out train schedules. When the Nazis seized Brest Litovsk, my grandfather, grandmother, and their youngest daughter, my mother's sister, were buried in a pit with others.

As my mother sat in the living room at night, waiting for my father to come home from work, she sometimes cried. This was my personal experience of the Holocaust, in a three-room apartment on the Lower East Side of Manhattan, amid claw-footed furniture covered by plastic to protect the fabric.

I had no concrete understanding of her grief. I'd never met my grandparents, uncles, or aunt. I had to imagine things—the story about my grandfather, the danger of streets . . . Eventually, I figured it was bad for Jews the way *it* is said to be raining. I didn't know what *it* was, only that *it* was worse than Hitler, older, absolutely unreasonable, strong, able to do things like fix the plumbing and paint the walls. *It* was like animals and trees, what lives outside, more physical than a person, though *it* appeared in persons. With this understanding, I was slow to perform simple, childhood actions—riding a bicycle, throwing a ball, running like other bodies—which expressed one's being-at-home-in-the-world.

My mother—without parents, siblings, friends, or English—was generally intimidated by America, even fearful of going out alone in the streets. She had black hair which she wore in long braids. Her eyes were blue. Strange men wanted to approach and talk to her. She kept me close. We were constantly together. Her many fears nourished mine, especially because I was sickly, susceptible to respiratory diseases and ear infections; colds, bronchitis, pleurisy, and pneumonia twice. Through feverish delirium, I heard my mother at my bedside saying, *"Meir far deir,"* which means: Let me die rather than you. Her phrase, repeated like a radio signal, kept me from drifting out of life.

I learned English, mainly from the woman who lived next door. Her name was Lynn Nations. She came from Texas and was married to a Jew, Arthur Kleinman, a furrier and lefty intellectual. They had no children. She worked at Saks Fifth Avenue, a tall, slender woman with fine features and light brown hair. She was proud of her legs, and she flaunted a tough, classy manner. I remember the clack of her high heels on the marble floor of the outside hallway. I was often in her apartment and she in ours, telling us the smart things she'd said that day at Saks, how she corrected her customers' taste and sold them half the store. We understood her idea of herself, if not always what she said, but she talked at us for years, teasing us toward English. To her, my Yiddish was hilarious. "Arthur, did you hear what he called the telephone wire? A *shtrik*. No wonder he's afraid of it."

Arthur, fluent in Yiddish, looked at me with astonishment. "*Das iz nisht a shtrik. Das iz a telephone vyeh.*" I see his Slavic face leaning down, thick in nose and lip, winking at me, compromising English and Yiddish to assure me that meaning is greater than words.

When I came crying from the playground after some kid hit me, Lynn's eyes contracted into icy dots of rage. She snatched me from my mother by the back of my neck—"You let go of your child"—and steered me into the playground and thrust me toward the kid. Still crying, I started swinging, and it was good, it was excellent, for a scrawny sickly kid to hear his blubbering become curses and to be a piece of nature in a playground fistfight. Lynn hated my crying, seeing it as pogrom-obsessed *Yiddishkeit*. For her better opinion, I made small beginnings, used my fists, spoke English. During the war I changed further.

I put a big map of Europe on my bedroom wall. When I read about Allied bombing raids in Germany, Italy, or elsewhere, I found the city and stuck a red pin into it. I imagined myself a B-17 pilot or bombardier. In movies, I saw the doors of the bomb bay swing open and long bombs with tails and sticklike incendiaries fall away toward factories, railroad tracks, and whole cities. This great work was being done by regular guys from America. My mother took me to the movies on Friday afternoons after school. Before we left, I had to drink a glass of milk. I hated its whiteness, the whiteness of its taste. "Finish the whole glass. It's good for you." But then came the B-17, struck with machine guns in ribs, nose, belly, and tail, a primordial reptile dragging long flaps and lugubrious claws for landing gear, lumbering up into the gray dawn among its thousand sisters, each bearing a sacred gift of bombs.

After the war, her brothers' names appeared in the *Forward*, published a few blocks from us, in a white building opposite the Seward Park Library that I'd passed many times on the way to my father's barbershop around the corner on Henry Street. The distant, the exotic, the fairy tale of evil and a murdered family was suddenly in these familiar streets, even in the Garden Cafeteria near the foot of the *Forward* building, where I sometimes sat with my father and ate whitefish on black bread with onion, amid the dark Jewish faces of taxi drivers, pickle salesmen, dry-goods merchants, journalists, and other urban beings who sipped coffee or borscht, and smoked cigarettes and argued, joked, or complained in Yiddish, or in such English as had been mutilated into the nuances required by Yiddish, grammatical niceties flung aside so that meaning and feeling could walk on the earth.

The names of my uncles, Yussel and Srulke Czeskies, had appeared among those of survivors gathered in camps for displaced persons who now sought relatives in America. One uncle had been in the Russian army, the other in the Polish army. I was happy. I was also worried. Would my mother be held responsible for what they had endured? When her brothers actually stood in our apartment, I retreated to corners, absorbed in shadowy thought, like a neighborhood cat. A strange mechanism of feeling drew me from happiness toward internal complications; early notions of guilt as fundamental to life.

The father of a friend of mine developed his own religious practices, reducing life to secret study and his tuxedo-renting business. He was a big gloomy man with a high rounded back, black brows, and a reproachful glare. During the day, he worked. At night, he studied. He sought the deepest meaning of things, the fate of the Jews. There had been a tragic mistake. He would discover, in holy books, how to understand the Holocaust.

Even as a child, I thought Jews were obsessed with meaning. We didn't just eat, sleep, work, study, play, but needed the meaning of these things and everything. Meaning as such, as if it had practical value, like wood or gold. We sought it with brain fingers, loved how it feels in the elaborations of talk. At the heart of all meaning was the religion, the law, forever established, yet open to perpetual analysis and explication. But I knew that beneath all meaning was the general complicity with murder. In the sidewalks, the grass, the weather, and the human heart: the need to murder.

And yet, outside, in murderous nature, I could see that colors never clash and the world is everywhere beautiful. I feared its allure.

I remember pictures of President Roosevelt, the long handsome face with its insouciant smile, his cigarette holder aloft in a white aristocratic hand, perhaps in the manner of SS officers outside the windows of the gas chambers, chatting and smoking as we died in agony visible to them. Of course, I wasn't there. I had only a sense of ubiquitous savagery, the inchoate, nightmarish apprehensions of a child, much like insanity or the numinousness of a religious vision where ideas have the force of presence, overriding logic. Yiddish-speaking relatives discussed the President's tepid reaction to Kristallnacht and his decision to turn away a ship of Jewish refugees from American shores. From those who could make a difference, I figured, came indifference. Knowing nothing about immigration laws or the isolationist politics of America, I understood only a weird mixture of comfort and sadism in the President's smile. In his capacity to do something lived the frisson of doing nothing. I couldn't have articulated this understanding any more than I could have said how I tie my shoelaces.

"Take care," writes Primo Levi, "not to suffer in your own homes what is inflicted on us here." He means don't let his experience of Auschwitz become yours. I read the sentence repeatedly before I understood that is all he

means, and that he doesn't mean: DON'T FEEL THESE
THINGS IN THE DAILINESS OF YOUR LIFE OR IT WILL POISON
EVERYTHING ELSE—running in the playground, speaking
English, knowing it's time to make a fist.

Thus, misreading a few words, I rediscover my primi-
tive apprehensions long after the Holocaust. I literally
remind myself that I wasn't with my grandparents in
Poland, or with the children packed into cattle trains to
the death camps. I can't claim too little. Nothing happened to me. I was a sickly kid, burdened by sweaters
and scarves and winter coats buttoned to the neck. If I
loosened my scarf or undid a coat button, my mother
would fly into a state of panic, as though millions of
germs were shooting through the gap I'd made in my
clothing.

Literary Talk

§ About forty years ago, in a high-school English class, I learned that talking about literature is like talking about yourself but literary talk is logical and polite, a social activity of nice people. My teacher's name was McLean, a thin man with a narrow head and badly scarred tissue about his mouth, which was obscured by a mustache, British and military-looking. The scar tissue was plain enough, despite the mustache, like crinkled wrapping paper with a pink sheen. Listening to him, looking at his face, I heard his voice as crushed; softly crushed by the grief around his mouth. He'd been in the air force. I supposed it happened during the war.

McLean usually wore an old brown tweed suit and a dull appropriate tie, and he had a gentle, formal manner, nearly timid. Whenever he made some little joke, he chuckled nervously, as though he'd gone too far, exceeding the propriety of the classroom. Telling jokes calls attention to your mouth; his for sure. Some days, as if sensitive to weather, the scar tissue looked raw, hot, incompletely healed.

Long before McLean's class, I knew the strong effects of stories and poems, but through him I discovered you could talk about the effects as if they inhered in the words, just as his voice inhered in his face. When McLean read poetry aloud, his voice became vibrant and the air of the classroom seemed full of pleasure, feeling its way into me with my breathing.

One afternoon, discussing *The Winter's Tale*, McLean came to a passage I didn't like. Paulina and Dion debate whether or not King Leontes should remarry. Years ago, deranged by evil jealousy, Leontes practically murdered his former queen, Hermione. Paulina says to Dion, "You are one of those / Would have him wed again." Dion replies:

> *What were more holy*
> *Than to rejoice the former queen is well?*
> *What holier than . . .*
> *To bless the bed of majesty again*
> *With a sweet fellow to't?*

The queen is dead, long live the queen. All in all, Dion's speech imagines the dead queen alive, blessing "the bed of majesty again," in another woman's body, which will restore "a sweet fellow to't." The "to't," like a bird belching rather than tweeting, seemed to me disgusting, and Dion's whole speech, conflating a real dead woman and an imagined living one, was very creepy. I raised my hand. McLean looked at me. I said, "Necrophilia."

McLean asked me to stay after class, then went on, enraptured by the moment when Hermione steps out of the stone statue of herself and back into the living world. But I could think only that Leontes, much older now than the long-dead Hermione—their daughter being grown up and marriageable—can look forward to going to bed with Hermione again, making love to her. Old Evil eating innocence, as in a black vision of Goya. Poor Hermione, tragically abused, would now be debauched by Leontes, criminal psychopath, her husband. I wouldn't accept the idea of her statue showing her as aged. Wouldn't see it. Couldn't.

After class, everyone left the room but McLean and me. I went up to his desk. He fooled with papers. He couldn't simply turn and say what was on his mind. Too direct. He collected papers, ordered them, collecting himself. I was scared. I was always scared. Not a good student, I didn't feel morally privileged to receive McLean's attention—alone; this close. It was hard for me even to raise my hand amid the pool of heads, then speak. I'd go deaf when McLean responded and I'd sit nodding like a fool, understanding nothing, hearing nothing, the blood noisy in my head and my tie jumping to my heartbeat. Though barely perceptible, it could be seen.

Still looking at his papers, McLean said, "Some people make a practice of burying their dead quickly and getting on with life." My people, presumably. I didn't know why he said that, but I took the distinction without resentment. He was thinking out loud, unable to talk to me otherwise, perhaps too embarrassed by what he wanted to say, or his inability to say it. Then he said, "I was a ball-turret gunner." He was telling me a story.

Ball-turret gunners, in the belly of a B-17, the most vulnerable part, were frequently killed. McLean said he would become terrified in action. He'd spin and spin the turret, firing even when the German fighter planes were out of range. He gazed at me, but his eyes weren't engaging mine, perhaps seeing a vast and lethal sky, the earth whirling below in flames. On his last mission he was ordered to replace the side gunner of another B-17, who had been killed. It was the worst mission he'd ever flown. The B-17 was hit repeatedly. It lost an engine, the landing gear was destroyed, and it was going to crash-land on its belly. The man in the ball turret had to get out, but there was mangled steel above him. He couldn't move; he was trapped. As they went down, McLean bent over him. He looked up at McLean. "His eyes were big," said McLean. "Big."

I felt myself plummet through the dark well of my body. McLean's eyes were big, big. In that moment of utter horror, he whispered, "It's a great play, *The Winter's Tale.* Can you believe me?"

———

The Abandoned House

§ I lived with two other graduate students, Jay Norden and David Forest, down by the railroad tracks, half a mile from the University of Michigan campus, in a house that had only a stove, a refrigerator, and three mattresses, one for each bedroom. We slept on the mattresses on the floor. In the morning we fled the house and went to classes. In the evening we met in a bar called The Ideal, a very dark place with a grim erotic mood. Until closing time, we drank with friends. Then we walked back to the house. Months passed. The house remained hollow. Passing freight trains filled the empty rooms with banging iron. Our voices, magnified by emptiness, were loud; our laughter sounded hysterical. It was a bleak and uncomfortable way to live and, since we ate meals out, expensive. We didn't have a coffeepot. We didn't have a cup or a spoon. We didn't because we didn't. I don't know why. There was no pleasure in such deprivation, or in the cold bare floors and walls. One night at The Ideal, a bartender said he knew of an abandoned house fifteen miles outside of town. Full of furniture. He drew us a map on a paper napkin.

"It's like salvaging goods from a sunken ship," said Norden, a shrewd light in his eyes, yellowish, small, set high in the long blade of his face. A narrow nose, pointed mouth, front teeth slightly exposed, ratlike. He nodded yes-yes-yes to Forest and me. His mathematician's mind, very quick, was reflected in his skinny, nervous body, everywhere jerky and impulsive. He'd reach for his beer glass and knock it over. He'd walk into doorjambs and the sharp edge of things. He was otherwise unlucky, too, always losing important stuff—eyeglasses, fountain pen, wallet, notebooks. His girlfriend's dog bit him on the mouth. He rode his bicycle over a sewer grate. The front wheel caught, flinging him across the handlebars into the street. He stood up with torn hands and knees, laughing. Gifted in math but a complete *shlimazel*. The more he wanted to go, the more it felt unwise, unlucky. I offered no opinion and waited for Forest.

He had a different ethos. Big-boned, blond, a wide face, sleepy gray eyes, and a slow heavy mouth. He could read five languages, and he spoke them all in a whiny Boston accent; a squeal almost, surprising in a big man. His German could pass for his Spanish. He looked up from the bartender's map, then left his bar stool and walked toward the street door, carrying himself with judicious dignity, anticipating the day when he'd be bigger and heavier and read ten languages. "I'll fetch my flashlight," he said. "Borrow the landlord's pickup, Norden. Meet us at home." He assumed we'd follow him into the street. We did.

Driving in the warm October night beneath a yellow moon, Norden at the wheel, I saw flat shining fields and scattered stands of oak and pine fly past on either side. The house was where the bartender's map said it would be, floating like a black barge in a lake of black grass, a hundred feet from the road. Two stories, bungalow-style; an external chimney and an enclosed front porch.

The moonlight was strong. No clouds. Forest didn't use his flashlight, since it could be seen miles away and the countryside was patrolled. We trudged in tall grass, stumbled into ruts. Vegetables had once been planted here. The earth was stonelike now, the grass stiff, splintery. Norden jumped onto the porch and strode to the door. "Nailed shut," he said. He began kicking it. Forest and I stepped onto the porch, forced a window up, and slid beneath the sash. Norden stopped kicking.

In palpable gloom, we stood together trying to sense the proportions of the parlor. Moonlight, cut off by the thrust of the porch roof, didn't enter the room. My skin, sensitized by darkness, took incomprehensible messages, but I knew something in front of us was large. Forest turned on his flashlight. "Nobody move."

We saw a black hole at our feet. One step plunged us. Forest traced the edge of the hole with his light and poked into the center. The beam caught an object. Smashed, spewing wires like an explosive disembowelment, keys streaming along a jumbled, twisted line—an upright piano in the bottom of the hole, obscene and tragic-looking. The floor had collapsed, dropping it through the rug, trailing hairy streamers of wool.

Forest moved the light away. Blackness gobbled piano. Forest's light then discovered a sofa, a highboy, chairs, standing lamps, framed portrait-photographs, and a door. We edged around the hole, then through the door into a kitchen with a brick floor and a high, square, five-legged farm table in the center. Four plates and mugs, with knives, forks, and spoons, had been set. A newspaper lay folded across one plate. A family was about to arrive, sit, eat breakfast. It suggested memorial statuary, pure waiting, without any expectation.

I stayed close behind Norden, he behind Forest, who led us back through the parlor and around the piano-hole to a staircase. In a second-floor bedroom stood a double bed with a tall walnut headboard, leafy design across the top. Whoever carved it had good hands; good feeling for sleep. The high dark wood invited you to lie down as if beneath a mighty tree. A quilt of silky pieces lay on the bed, lavenders, silvers, and grays. It had a religious feeling, sensuous, muted, very serious. I didn't want to touch anything, let alone take. "We'll take that dresser and go," said Norden. No enthusiasm in his voice, only anxiety to get it over with; get out.

Forest stepped to a dresser opposite the bed. "Not

heavy." It was heavy. Solid maple. Lifting together, we shuffled out of the bedroom to the stairs, Norden at the front, me in the middle, my spine sliding along the banister. Halfway down, the dresser jammed. Forest, above me, took the weight on his knees. Norden pressed up from below, weight against his chest. "Lift higher," he said, "free it." The baseboard stabbed through the slickness of my palms, seeking bone. Forest, wheezing, heaved left and right. "Come on, free it." The dresser was adamant. My legs trembled. My neck swelled with heat and pressure. I wanted to kick the son-of-a-bitch. Then, with imperceptible suddenness, the dresser became weightless and the darkness closed in, embraced us softly, affectionately, as if to say, "I know you're really good boys."

I was keen as a cat. Forest whispered, "Did you hear it?"

I let go, slithering free of the dresser before it crashed. Forest hurtled downstairs on hands and knees. The back of Norden's shirt in my fist, I swerved with him at the hole. Forest was right behind me, shoving my back as I dove behind Norden through the space at the bottom of the window. We hit the porch and scrambled into the field, running. Grass lashed my legs like wires. Struggling against his bulk, Forest made speed for a big man.

In the cab of the pickup, Norden slapped his pockets. "Lost the key." Forest punched the dashboard with his thick fist, as if not to punch him. I saw the key sticking out of the ignition cylinder and said, "There." Norden's hand twisted it. His other hand flicked on the headlights. The engine lurched. The road leaped at us.

None of us knew what we'd heard in the farmhouse.

In the days that followed, we went to local junk shops and bought a couch, kitchen table, rug, and curtains. Then we had a coffeepot, cups, spoons, and food in the refrigerator. We ate breakfast at home. Cups, spoons, knives, forks; all different shapes and sizes plucked off shelves and scooped out of bins. They clattered against the porcelain of the sink and felt good being soaped. Lingering at the kitchen table on a winter morning, I listened to a freight train banging and clanking by. When it had passed, I listened to silence. No less definite. Sparrows twittered just outside the window, but I continued to hear, beyond them, a universe of silence, intolerant of intrusions before the moment assigned.

Sylvia

§ In 1960, after two years of graduate school at Berkeley, I returned to New York without a Ph.D. or any idea what I'd do, only a desire to write stories. I'd also been to graduate school at the University of Michigan, from 1953 to 1956, which came to five years of classes in literature, and I wasn't a scholar or a writer or anything but an overspecialized man, twenty-seven years old, who could give no better account of himself than to say "I love to read." It doesn't qualify the essential picture, but I had a lot of friends, got along with my parents, and women liked me. In a vague and happy way, I felt humored by the world, and whatever my predicament, I wasn't yet damaged by judgment, though I inflicted it on myself every minute. I had nothing else to do.

A few days after arriving in New York, I went to see Naomi Kane, a good pal from the University of Michigan. We'd spent innumerable hours together drinking coffee in the Student Union, center of romantic social life and general sloth. She lived in Greenwich Village, on MacDougal Street near the corner of Bleecker. From my parents' Lower East Side neighborhood, I rode the F train, which went shrieking through the rock bowels of Manhattan to the West Fourth Street station. Then I walked.

It was a hot Sunday afternoon in June. Village streets carried slow, turgid crowds of sightseers, especially MacDougal, a main drag between Eighth Street and Bleecker, the famous Eighth Street Bookshop at one end, the famous San Remo bar at the other. I'd walked it thousands of times during my high-school days, when I'd gone with a girl who lived in the Village, and later all through college, when I'd gone with another who lived in the Village. But I'd been away for two years. I hadn't seen MacDougal Street change, becoming jammed with new stores and coffeehouses, and I hadn't felt the new apocalyptic atmosphere. Around then, Elvis Presley and Allen Ginsberg were the kings of feeling, and the word *love* was like a proclamation with the force of *kill*. I saw a blunt admonition chalked on the wall of the subway station: FUCK HATE. Weird delirium was in the air and in the sluggish, sensual crowds as I pressed toward the sooty-faced tenement where Naomi lived.

The street door had no lock or buzzer. I pushed in, into a long and narrow hallway, painted with greenish enamel that had a dingy, fishy glare. It ran straight through the building to the door of a coffeehouse called

Sylvia

The Fat Black Pussy Cat. Urged by the oppression of the walls, hardly a foot from either shoulder, I walked quickly. Just before the coffeehouse, I came to a stairway with a black iron banister. I climbed six flights, then walked down a darker, narrower hallway. Brittle waves of old linoleum crackled beneath my steps. Naomi's door, like the entrance to an office, had a clouded glass window. I knocked. She opened and, with a great hug, welcomed me into a small living room dominated by a raw brick wall. The floor was thick, wide, rough, unfinished planks, as in a warehouse. Light fell through two tall windows; one looked west to New Jersey; the other east, across MacDougal Street, to tenements like this one where Italian families lived. Naomi said, "Don't make any wisecracks. The rent is forty bucks a month." Then she introduced me to her roommate, Sylvia Bloch, who minutes earlier had stepped down out of the shower, which was a metal stall in the kitchen, elevated beside the sink.

Sylvia said hello while brushing her hair with deep slashing strokes, tipping her head right and left, tossing the wet black weight. Then she quit and dropped onto the couch, brush still in hand, as if she'd never move again. The question of what to do with my life was resolved for the next four years.

Sylvia was slender and very tan. Straight, black, dense, shining hair fell below the middle of her back. Low bangs, obscuring her eyes, made her look shy or modestly hiding, and also shorter than she was. She was about five six. Behind the bangs her eyes, black as her hair, seemed quick and brilliant. She had a long fine neck, wide shoulders, narrow hips, delicately shaped wrists and ankles; a figure and face like Egyptian statuary. She wore a light cotton Indian dress with an intricate flowery print, the same brown hue as her skin.

We sat in the living room until Naomi's date arrived, and then we went out, staying loosely together, strolling against the slow pressure of the crowd, heading up Mac-Dougal Street toward Washington Square Park. Naomi walked alongside me and whispered, "She's not beautiful, you know." It was obvious that I'd been hypnotized by Sylvia's flashing exotic effect. I felt embarrassed and took the remark seriously, but I didn't wonder if Sylvia was beautiful. Naomi then said, "Well, she is very smart."

We were supposed to have dinner together and maybe go to a movie, but Naomi and her date disappeared, abandoning Sylvia and me in the park. Neither of us was talking. We'd become social liabilities, too stupid with feeling to be fun. We continued on, as if dazed, drifting through dreamy heat. We'd met less than an hour ago, yet it seemed we'd been together, in the plenitude of this moment, forever. Neither of us was flirtatious; barely glancing at each other, staying close. Eventually, we turned back toward the tenement, with no reason, no plan, just slowly turning back through the crowded streets, then into the dismal green hall and up six flights of stairs, and into the squalid apartment, like a couple doomed to a sacrificial assignation. It started without beginning. We made love until afternoon became twilight and twilight became black night.

Through the tall, open window of the living room we saw the night sky and heard people proceed along Mac-Dougal Street, as in a lunatic carnival, screaming, breaking glass, wanting to hit, needing meanness. Someone played a guitar in another apartment. Someone was crying. Lights flew across the walls and ceiling. Radios were loud. The city made its statement in the living room. None of it had to do with us, lying naked on the couch, just wide enough for two, against the brick wall. Released by sex into simple confidence, Sylvia talked, answering my questions.

She was nineteen. She'd left the University of Michigan without taking a degree. Some years earlier, her father, who worked for the Fuller Brush Company, died of a heart attack. The doctors told him not to smoke. Her mother was a housewife who did well playing the stock market as a hobby. Soon after her husband's death, she died of cancer. Sylvia went to the hospital every day after high school. She said her mother became exquisitely sensitive as she declined, until even the odor of the telephone cord beside her bed nauseated her. After her mother died, Sylvia lived with an aunt and uncle in Queens. She had bad dreams; she heard voices. To get out of New York, she applied to the University of Michigan and Radcliffe. Her boyfriend was at Harvard. She described him as very kind and nice-looking, lean, fine-featured, blond. She was brighter than her boyfriend, but Radcliffe refused her. They could easily fill every class with German Jews. Nevertheless, Sylvia took the refusal personally. That was the end of her boyfriend. Her new boyfriend worked in a local restaurant. A tall, sweet, handsome Italian. He would show up tonight, she said. His swimsuit was in the apartment.

She was telling me how she'd met Naomi, how much she adored her, but I was thinking now of the boyfriend who would show up tonight. I wanted to go. Sylvia wouldn't let me. She got up and searched the apartment, found the swimsuit, and hung it on the doorknob outside the apartment by the jock. We lay in the loud, balmy darkness, whispering, waiting for him to arrive. After a while we heard his trudge on the stairway and along the linoleum hall to the door, the sound of a man who had worked all day. From the weight of his steps I figured he could break my head. The steps ended at the door, less than ten feet from us. No knock followed. He'd seen his swimsuit. He was contemplating it, reading its message. I supposed he wasn't stupid, but even a genius might kick in the door and make a moral scene. He said, "Sylvia?" His voice carried fatigue and pain, no righteousness. We lay still, disintegrated in the darkness. Moments passed. Again the question: "Sylvia?" Then his steps went away, but his voice stayed with me. I was sorry for him, and I felt responsible for his disappointment. Mainly, I was struck by Sylvia's efficiency, exchanging one man for another.

Would it happen to me, too? But she lay beside me now and the cruel uncertainty of love was only a moody flavor. We turned to each other renewed by the drama of betrayal. Afterwards, Sylvia sat naked on the window ledge, outlined against the western skyline of the city and the lights of Jersey. She stared at me lying in the darkness, and she seemed to collect a power of decision, or to wonder what decision had been made. Years later, in fury, she would say, "The first time we went to bed. The first time . . ." resurrecting the memory with bitterness, saying we'd done extreme things and I'd made her do them.

At dawn, having slept not one minute, we went down into the street. The residue of night, strewn along the curb and overflowing trash cans, was shining and beginning to stink in the early light. Broken, heaving sidewalks oozed moisture and a steamy glow. There was no traffic, no people. Between dark and day, the city stood in stunned, fetid slumber, deeply used. On a bench, in a small grassy area set back from Sixth Avenue, we sat staring into each other's eyes, unashamedly adoring, yet with a degree of reserve, or belated concern to see whom we'd been to bed with for the last ten hours.

Sylvia then said she was leaving for summer school at Harvard the next day. I thought of her former boyfriend and felt jealous, though I had no claim on her fidelity and perhaps didn't want it. She'd said she liked his blond looks, his gentle and Gentile old-money manners. I supposed I would lose her to him. Then she asked if I would come up to Cambridge and live with her. Her face was held high, stiff with anticipation, as if to receive a blow.

I see her. Maybe I know what I'm looking at.

I was taken by highlights along her cheekbones and the luscious expectancy in her lower lip. She waited for my answer. I liked the Asian cast of her face, its smoothness, length, and the tilt of its bones. Straight black hair against a look of cool dark blood. She was afraid I wouldn't say yes.

§ A week later I took the train to Boston. Sylvia moved out of her dormitory. We found a room near the university in a big house with many shadowy passages.

I took the train. We found a room . . .

The truth is, I didn't know what I was doing exactly, or why I was in Cambridge. Sylvia wanted me to be there. I had no reason to be elsewhere—no job, nothing to do. My desire to write stories, I believed, was nothing to do. It wouldn't pay. It wasn't work. When I looked at Sylvia's face, I liked what I saw, but I was sure of little. My feelings were as strong as they were uncertain.

The house was full of heavy, stolid things with sheets thrown over them. Blinds were drawn, doors shut, defending against light and air. A man in his sixties lived in the house amid the looming white masses and shadows.

Our room, on the second floor, held a mahogany

dresser, two lavishly upholstered chairs, and a giant bed. All wood surfaces were veneered in hard slick brown. Pulling back the bedcovers demanded a strong grip and snap. Sheets were tucked in tight, making a hard flat field, perfect for a corpse. The mattress, unusually thick, like a fat luxurious heart, was sealed, lashed down by bedcovers and the sheets.

When we came downstairs in the morning, the man sat waiting in a high-backed chair in the parlor. He was bald, gaunt, lean as a plank. His long platter face stared at the floor between his knees, as if into a pool of sorrow.

"You two will have to go," he said, very terse, a command drawn from his strange hell of New England propriety and constipation. It had occurred to him, maybe, in the middle of the night, that Sylvia and I were touching, doing evils to each other's body, though we labored to be quiet, fucking with Tantric subtlety, measuring pleasure slow and slow, out of respect for his ethical domain. We went back up to our room, packed, made no fuss, and were soon adrift in the busy, hot, bright streets around Harvard Square, carrying our bags.

Sylvia refused to return to her dormitory, though we had no place to go if we stayed together. I couldn't reason with her, couldn't argue. The glorious summer day made things more difficult. Storefronts and windshields flashed threats. Everyone walked with energetic purpose. They belonged in Cambridge and were good. We'd been thrown into the street with our bags, a weight like blighted romance. We were bad. Then, after phoning friends, we learned about a house where three undergraduates lived, in a working-class neighborhood, far from the university. Maybe they'd rent us a room. We didn't phone them first. We went there.

It was an ugly falling-down sloppy happy house. One of the men, Clive Miller, began talking to Sylvia, the moment he saw her, in baby talk. She said, "Hello." He answered, "Hewo," with a goofy grin. She thought he was hilarious, and she loved being treated like a little girl in a house full of men. The others treated her the way Clive did, more or less. She inspired it: darkly sensuous; shy; hiding behind long bangs. There was one empty room in the house. Nobody said we couldn't have it.

In the mornings, Sylvia went to class and I tried to begin writing stories. The room, just off the kitchen, was noisy with refrigerator traffic and running water. Sylvia studied in a library on campus. At night, we had some irascible moments, heavy sighs, angry whispers, but the room was narrow, hot, and airless. There were also mosquitoes. Nothing personal. Through most of the slow, lovely summer, we were happy. Sylvia was taking a class in art history. We went to museums, and worked together on her papers.

One afternoon, sitting on the front steps, waiting for Sylvia to return from class, I spotted her far down the street, walking slowly. When she saw me looking at her, she walked more slowly. Her right sandal was flapping.

The sole had torn loose. At last she came up to me and showed me how a nail had poked through the sole. She had walked home on that nail, sole flapping, her foot sloshing in blood. What else could she do? She smiled wanly, suffering but good-spirited.

I said she could have had the sandal fixed or walked barefoot. There was something impatient in my voice. She seemed shocked. Her smile went from wan to screwy, perturbed, injured.

For days thereafter, Sylvia walked about Cambridge pressing the ball of her foot onto the nail, bleeding. She refused to wear other shoes. I argued with her. Finally, she let me take the sandal to be repaired. I was very grateful. She was not grateful. I was not forgiven.

§ *"Go, I don't love you. I hate you. I don't hate, I despise you. If you love me, you'll go. I think we can be great friends and I'm sorry we never became friends."*

"Can I get you something?"

"A menstrual pill. They're in my purse."

I found the little bottle and brought her a pill.

"Go now."

I lay down beside her. We slept in our clothes.

(Journal, December 1961)

§ At the end of the summer we returned to New York. Naomi moved out of the MacDougal Street apartment. I moved in with Sylvia. By then, fighting every day, we'd become ferociously intimate. Like a kid having a tantrum, she'd get caught up in the momentum of screaming. She had no desire to stop, maybe no way. She screamed because she screamed, building a universe of noise. All hers. She was boss. I found myself doing it, too, in response to her eyes and teeth, bright whites and blacks, and her contorted features. We sometimes went from fighting to sex. For me, a hideous new thrill. The fights always came in the middle of a trivial disagreement. Sylvia would begin to break things. I'd try to stop her. She would twist loose and come flying back at me, and then it became erotic; anyhow, sexual. Afterwards she slept. Neither of us mentioned what had happened. Ordinary or violent, sex was frequent and more exhausting than satisfying. Sylvia said she'd never had an orgasm, and, as if I were the one who stood between her and that ultimate pleasure, announced, "I will not live my whole life without an orgasm." She said she'd had several lovers better than I was.

§ I began trying to write again. Sylvia began taking classes at N.Y.U., a few blocks away across Washington Square Park, to complete her undergraduate work. She asked me what she ought to declare as her major. I said that if I were doing it over, I'd major in classics. I should have said nothing. She registered for Latin and Greek, ancient history, art history, and a class in eighteenth-century English literature. A maniacal program. She had to learn the complex grammars of two languages, read fat books, take exams, and write papers while living in squalor and fighting with me every day. I expected confusion and disaster, but she was abnormally bright and did well enough.

There was no desk in the apartment, but she didn't need the conveniences of students, didn't even notice their absence. She studied sitting on the edge of the bed in a mess of papers, doing the job, getting it over with. We also ate dinner in the bed, mainly noodles, frozen vegetables, and orange juice, or we went out for pizza or Chinese food. Neither of us cooked. My mother often gave us food. I'd carry it back to MacDougal Street after our visits two or three times a month. One night, after dinner, my mother slipped away to the bedroom with Sylvia's coat and sewed up a tear in the sleeve. As we were about to leave, she surprised Sylvia with the mended coat. Sylvia seemed grateful and affectionate. In the street, she became hysterical with indignation, feeling she'd been humiliated. Thereafter, I visited my parents alone.

I would always bring food back to MacDougal Street —fried chicken, steak, matzoh-ball soup, cookies. Sylvia would eat. Once, when I was at my parents' apartment, she phoned to say that she'd slit her wrists. She had refused to go with me, and she hadn't wanted me to go. I left in a hurry, but not before my mother had packed a bag with a dozen bagels, jars of gefilte fish, and a salad she made of onions and radishes. I didn't want to go rushing back, terrified by Sylvia's threats of self-destruction. Besides, I didn't believe she had really slit her wrists. But I couldn't be certain. In my frustration, I yelled at my mother for holding me as she packed the food. She probably suspected things were bad on MacDougal Street, but if I left without the food she'd know they were very bad. I didn't want her to know and I didn't want Sylvia to bleed to death, so I ran to the subway, and ran from the subway to our apartment, and I burst in hot and wild, the bag of food in my arms, shouting, "I don't give a damn if you slashed your neck."

She had sliced her wrists superficially. She'd done it once before we met and was good at it. There was a little bleeding. There'd be no scars. She began picking at the food. I felt relieved, hopeful. She liked gefilte fish. It pleased me to see her eat. There was hope for us if Sylvia ate gefilte fish, partaking of my mother's goodness. It was delicious, nothing to fight about, but she ate sullenly, as if conceding that there might be a reason to live.

§ Because of our fights, Sylvia often didn't begin studying until after midnight. Sitting on the edge of the bed, remains of dinner all about, she held a grammar book in her lap and flipped pages, glaring at the words as if they were a distraction from her real concern—me. She said I was "doing this" to her, starting fights, trying to ruin her chances, make her fail. She wasn't really interested in Latin and Greek, but she feared academic disgrace. She told me that when she was a kid she'd been accepted by the Hunter school for gifted children, and every morning, just before leaving for school, she would go into the bathroom and vomit. Nobody at the school knew that she lived in Queens, rather than Manhattan, where the students were required to live, and she feared discovery. At the end of the day, she'd ride the subway back to Queens and sometimes fall asleep and miss her stop. She'd wake up frightened, then catch a train going back, and when she got home she'd find her mother flat on the floor, her eyes shut, looking dead. It was only a joke—she'd died waiting for Sylvia—but it frightened her more than anything else.

I always thought Sylvia went much too fast, flipping through pages she couldn't have absorbed, then tossing the book aside and picking up another. She'd say as she studied, "You're doing this to make me fail"—like a chant, pages flying—and she'd say it again early in the morning as she flung out the door still wearing her clothes of the previous day, in which she'd slept, for maybe an hour, before leaving. Her long black hair bouncing and flying, blouse crumpled and half buttoned, skirt twisted on her hips, she hustled through the Village streets to N.Y.U., like a madwoman imitating a coed.

§ *We were sitting on the bed after dinner. I was looking at a magazine. Sylvia was beginning to study. I commented on the beauty of one of the models in an advertisement. Sylvia glanced at the photo, then said, "Your ideal of beauty is blue, slanted eyes."*

"So?"

Sylvia dropped backward on the bed, pulled the pillows against her ears, and began sobbing and thrashing. Then she stopped, sat up, and said, "I never went into detail about my sexual experiences."

I sat in silence and waited. She fell back again, made leering, hating faces, writhed like an epileptic, and then sat up and slapped my cheek and said, "I can't see why you don't adore me."

(Journal, December 1961)

§ In throes of hysteria, when it appeared she was totally out of control, her voice suddenly became cool and elegant, and she'd make a witty remark, as if every quality of the moment was clear to her—the hatefulness of her display as well as my startled appreciation of her wit. She was swept into hysteria as easily as she sometimes fell into sudden calm. I took this as a good sign, thinking it meant she wasn't really nuts. She felt the same way about it. "I know how I'm behaving," she'd say. But all in all, given the general misery of our daily life, it's remarkable that I didn't leave. In someone else, I'd consider my inability to get out contemptible and stupid, but she touched levels of aesthetic and sentimental disease in me. I'd think Sylvia's hysteria meant something I couldn't understand because I wasn't a good enough person, whereas she was a precious mechanism in which exceedingly fine springs and wheels had been brutally mangled. Anyhow, I was locked into some idea like that. I felt strong revulsion, but even as it became insufferable, it held me tighter. It would have been easy to leave her. Had it been difficult, I might have done it.

A main cause of our fights was my desire to get off the bed after dinner and go into the tiny room adjoining the living room. It contained a cot, a kitchen chair, and a shaky wooden typewriter table shoved against the tall window. There were only inches between the back of my chair and the cot. I sat at the table, looking out over the rooftops with their chimneys, clotheslines, and pigeon coops, toward the Hudson River and the Upper West Side. Wind rattled the glass, penetrating old loose putty, carrying icy air from the Hudson River to my fingers. They stiffened as I typed. My chin and the tip of my nose became numb. I'd hear Sylvia sigh and flip the pages of her books. I heard the sound of her pencil when she made notes. I was four steps away. Nevertheless, she'd feel excluded, lonely, angry. Only four steps away, but I was out of sight and not seeing her. She must have felt herself cease to exist.

After dinner I lingered with her on the bed, reading

a magazine as she collected notebooks, preparing to study. When she began, I'd begin to leave. Never in a simple, natural way; always with vague gradualness. I'd stir, lay aside the magazine, lean toward the cold room.

"Going to your hole?"

Sometimes I'd settle back onto the bed, thinking, "I'll write tomorrow when she's at school. Maybe she'll go to sleep in a few hours. I'll write then. A small sacrifice, better than a fight." That in itself—my desire not to fight —could be an incitement. "Why don't we discuss this for a minute . . ." To sound rational, when she was wrought up, wrought her up further, like a smack in the face. She once threw the typewriter she'd given me—"to help you write"—at my head. An Olivetti portable, Lettera 22. It struck a wall, then the floor, but was undamaged. I still use it. She also failed to destroy the telephone, though she tried many times, flinging it against the brick wall.

I wrote and I wrote, and I tore everything up, and I wrote some more. After a while I didn't know why I was writing. My original desire, complicated enough, became a grueling compulsion, partly in despite of Sylvia, as if I were doing hard work in the cold room, much harder than necessary, in the hope that it would justify itself. Sometimes, writing in the cold room, I'd become exhilarated, as if I'd transcended all difficulties. I'd done something good. A day later, rereading with a more critical eye, I would sink into the blackest notions of destiny. It was no good. I was no good.

"Going to your hole?"

I felt I was digging it.

§ *Sylvia had pain in her shoulder. She lay in bed and asked me to rub it, but when I touched her she squirmed spasmodically and pushed my hand away. I kept trying to do it right, but she wouldn't stop squirming and wouldn't tell me just where to rub. Then she lunged out of bed and paced the room, rubbing her shoulder herself.*

"I have a sore spot. A stranger could rub it better than you."

(Journal, January 1962)

§ Sylvia was often in pain or a nervous, defeated condition, especially when she got her period. She'd lie on the couch, our bed, groaning, whimpering, begging me to go buy her Tampax. I didn't see how it could ease her pain, but she was insistent, whining and writhing. She wanted Tampax. Needed Tampax. Long after midnight, I'd be out in the streets looking for an open drugstore. I dreaded the man at the counter, who would think I was an exceptionally bizarre Village transvestite. So I asked for Tampax in a hoodlumish voice, as if it were manufactured for brutal males. One night I detected the faintest smile on Sylvia's lips. Having me buy her Tampax turned her on. I decided to stop. As if she'd read my mind, she stopped asking.

§ I recorded our fights in a secret journal, because I was less and less able to remember how they started. There would be some insult, then disproportionate anger, and I would then feel I didn't know why this was happening. What had I done? What had I said? Sometimes I had the mysterious impression that the anger wasn't directed at me. I'd only stepped into the line of fire, the real target being long dead. Once, when I thought a bad scene was over, I lay down and threw my arm over my eyes. It was after 3 a.m., but Sylvia wouldn't turn off the light. She watched me from a chair, six feet from the bed. Then I heard her say, "I don't know how you find the courage to go to sleep." She might stick a knife in my heart, I supposed, if she could afford to kill me and be alone. Sleep took no courage at all. I wasn't afraid.

Another time she pulled my shirts out of the dresser and jumped up and down on them and spit on them. I seized her wrists and pressed her down on the bed while I screamed that I loved her. By tiny degrees, she seemed to relax, to relent. I urged her along, like a dance partner. More observer than committed fighter, I sensed the exact changes she passed through.

After a fight, unless there was sex, Sylvia usually collapsed into sleep. Ringing with anguish, very confused, terrifically awake, I began to force myself to rethink the fight, moment by moment, writing it all down in the cold room as Sylvia slept. It was my way of knowing, if nothing else, that this was really happening.

I hid the journal in a slot just below the surface of the table where I wrote stories. None of the stories was about life on MacDougal Street. I also never talked about it, and I imagined that nobody knew how bad things were. As a matter of high principle and shame, I kept it to myself. By sneaking the record of events into my journal, I made them even more secret. Then, one afternoon, Malcolm Raphael, an old friend from Michigan, visited. We were alone. He said he'd just come from Majorca, where he'd overheard some Americans, lying near him on the beach, talking about me and Sylvia. One of them lived in our building. He described our fights to the others, repeating what we screamed at each other. I felt myself going blind and deaf, repudiating the news, denying it in my physiology. Malcolm saw my reaction, laughed, and told me about fights he'd had with his wife. They were as bad, but he made them funny. He was unashamed.

I was grateful to him; relieved; almost giddy. Others lived this way, too, even a charming, sophisticated guy like Malcolm. We laughed together. I felt happily irresponsible. Countless men and women, I supposed, all over America, were tearing each other to pieces. I was normal. It was a great feeling, but to think this way gave me the creeps. I was thinking like some former acquaintances, flamboyant gay kids I'd met years ago, while learning how to skate at Iceland, the rink next to Madison Square Garden. I'd find them speeding about, slashing ice, or gathered at the edge watching other skaters and gossiping. They referred to everyone as a "faggot." The cop we passed in the street was a "cop-faggot." The mayor of New York was a "mayor-faggot." A famous football player was a "football-faggot." Every "he" was a "she." The more manly, strict, correct, moral, official, authoritative, the more faggot she.

My life with Sylvia—every couple, every marriage—was sick. We weren't yet married, but she wanted to do it soon.

§ Now, like the gay kids—shame notwithstanding—I was on stage, subject to the voracious curiosity of everybody. This experience, like bloodletting, purged me. I was miserably normal; I was normally miserable. What others thought—or I imagined they thought—I could think of them. No better defense than contempt. Nothing easier to give. It is a perverse generosity. Sylvia knew nothing about the gossip. Since she lived in constant dread of humiliation, I didn't tell her that our cover had been blown. It strengthened my commitment to her.

§ Like anyone else, I was affected by cultural radiations from newspapers, radios, and what walked the city streets, but my life was Sylvia. I had no place to go and forget her for a little while, and no one to be with whom Sylvia didn't imagine was her enemy. Once, hurrying back to the apartment from a twenty-minute meeting with a friend in the San Remo bar, a hundred feet from our building, I opened the apartment door on madness. Sylvia, at the stove, five feet away, turned toward me holding a plate of spaghetti in her hand—already startling, since she never cooked—and the plate came sailing toward my face, strands of spaghetti in the air untangling like a ball of snakes. Dinner! I caught it against my forearm.

The telephone, if it rang for me, was also her enemy. She'd say, "His master's voice," and hand me the phone. After I put it down, she'd jeer, "You love Bernie, don't you?" He was a witty guy. I'd laughed too hard at his remarks. Eventually, when answering the phone—if Sylvia was in the room—I kept my voice even and dull, or edged with annoyance, as if the call were tedious. I learned to talk in two voices, one for the caller, the other for Sylvia listening nearby in the tiny apartment.

Her friends, as opposed to mine, were sacrosanct, but I didn't mind them. I was glad when they phoned or visited. They proved Sylvia was lovable. I wanted her to have lots of friends, but she was carefully selective and soon got rid of her prettiest girlfriends, keeping only those who didn't remind her of her physical imperfections. In a department store, if the saleslady said a dress was too long for Sylvia, it was a comment on her repulsive shortness. If the saleslady said bright yellow was wrong for Sylvia, it was a judgment on her repulsive complexion. She would drag me quickly out into the street, saying that I thought the same as the saleslady.

"Why don't you admit it? You think I'm a pig."

If the saleslady was affectionate and sincerely attentive, Sylvia would buy anything. For every hundred dollars she spent on clothes, she got about fifty cents in value, and would have done better, at much less cost, in a Salvation Army thrift shop, blindfolded.

§ My mother's way of trying to help was to send food. My father's way was silence and looks of sad philosophical concern, but he also gave money. The time I tried, in a fugue of confessional incoherence, to tell him something about my life, he cut me off, saying, "She's an orphan. You cannot abandon her." An emotional coward, he couldn't bear listening, and I couldn't bear telling, so he made a pronouncement from the heavens and told me tales about husbands who suffered the lunacy of wives. I got the point. Nothing could or should be done. The couple is an absolute relation, immutable as the sea and the shore. I found myself lonely, wretched, and confused, and I began to wonder about seeing a psychiatrist. Toward the end of our life on MacDougal Street, I went to a psychiatrist reputed to be a decent guy, who listened for about half an hour, then heard something crucial and said, "Has she started calling you a homosexual?" I told him about the Tampax. He said this is

very serious and Sylvia ought to be committed. If I'd
sign papers, he'd do the rest. He followed me to the head
of the stairs, calling after me, "This is very serious." I
felt confirmed in my suspicions and was very high as I
ran to the subway, sobbing a little, running back to my
madwoman. I'd been strengthened by new, positive
knowledge, and a sense of connection to the wisdom of
our healing institutions. As a result, nothing changed.

§ One evening, after another long fight, Sylvia went
raging out of the apartment to take an exam in Greek,
saying she would fail, she had no hope of passing, she
would fail disgracefully, it was my fault, and "I will get
you for this." The door slammed. I sat on the bed listening to her footsteps hurry down the hall, then down the
stairs. I was immobilized by self-pity, but in a spasm of
strange determination, I got up, went out the door, and
followed her through the streets to N.Y.U. I stood outside her exam room and looked in. She sat in the back,
still wearing her thin, brown-leather, wraparound winter
coat, its tall collar standing higher than her ears. The
coat was nothing against a New York winter, but she
thought she looked great in it and wore it constantly. She
was bent, huddled over the questions, as if the exam
delivered heavy blows to her shoulders and the top of
her head. Her ballpoint pen, clutched in a bloodless fist,
moved very quickly, her face close to the page, breathing
on her words. Five minutes after the hour, she surren-

dered the paper to her professor and came out of the room with a yellowish face, looking killed. When she saw me, she came to me, whispering that she had been humiliated, had failed, it was my fault. But her tone was not reproachful. She was glad to find me waiting for her. I put my arm around her. She let me kiss her. We walked home together.

Her exam was the best in the class, and the professor urged her to persist in classical studies. She didn't always do that well; but considering how we lived, it was a miracle she passed anything. She took no pride in her success and never exhibited her learning in conversation, never referred to it. She was never basically interested; only performing. Academic achievements, to her, were an embarrassment.

"I'd give thirty points off my I.Q. for a shorter nose."

"Nothing is wrong with your nose."

"It's too long, a millimeter too long."

§ Agatha Seaman, who lived in Yonkers and visited Sylvia regularly, told her about a doctor in Switzerland who would reshape her nose without surgery, molding it by hand over a period of weeks at his clinic in the Alps. Sylvia cared less about the shape of her nose than its length, but she yearned for the mythical doctor. He'd been mentioned in a fashion magazine, said Agatha, as the darling of European society. Sylvia was resentful of Agatha, because she could easily afford to spend weeks at the Alpine clinic, whereas Sylvia couldn't. Not that she would go if she could afford it, but she wanted to believe there was such a doctor and that hope existed for her nose. I offered no opinions. None of it sounded kosher. I thought Sylvia wanted to do to her nose what she did to her dresses, which was constantly to change their length or width, or remove a collar or add a collar or tighten the shoulders. She always ruined them. There were dozens of dresses and skirts stuffed in boxes; none fit her like any other. She wore only a few things regularly. Everything else—dresses, skirts, blouses, sweaters for every occasion—was jammed into boxes in the back of closets or into suitcases that were never opened. Since she often fell asleep in her clothes, she'd wear the same things for days, while hundreds of pieces of clothing, altered and realtered, were never worn. I was happy with her nose and hoped she'd never change it, and I thought Agatha's doctor, like her life, was an extravagant fantasy irrelevant to Sylvia. Agatha's life had mainly to do with boys.

She was subject to degrading fixations on boys younger than she, poor, ignorant, dark—Arab, Turk, Italian, Puerto Rican—sublimely handsome, invariably vicious. If they weren't vicious before they met Agatha, she helped them discover it in themselves. I heard about them, month after month. She would tell Sylvia stories, sprawling for hours on our couch, always about the boys —how last night she waited in the alley behind the hotel where Abdul or Francisco or Julio worked as a bellhop or busboy, and when he appeared after work, she surprised him. The boys were outraged by these surprises, but Agatha always brought gifts—jewelry, leather jackets, beautiful shirts—tickets of admission to their lives. Trembling with humility and fear, she held the gift forth. The boy, unable to reject it, relented. She'd then follow him down the street as he fondled the gift, maybe tried it on. She whimpered about how gorgeous he looked wearing her gift. Gradually his anger gave way to a different feeling, and he would lead Agatha into a doorway or phone booth where he might allow her to blow him. Sometimes he'd turn her around and abuse her from behind, then leave her burning and bleeding and go meet his real date. "A mean selfish bitch," said Agatha. She said what the boys did to her with remarkable matter-of-factness, and never noticed that her stories were always the same—her passion, gifts, degradation, abandonment.

She might have been a gift sufficient in herself—a slender blonde about the same size and shape as Sylvia —but she indulged an enervated, unattractive manner. Her voice, kept low and dull to suggest sensitive feminine reserve, suggested a low-voltage brain and morbidity. Her complexion, embalmed for years in cosmetic chemicals, had the texture of tofu.

Contempt, pity, fascination, and affection bound Sylvia to Agatha. I liked her, too. The sickly languid manner, the air of fear and injury, had the appeal of a doomed kitten. Nobody was more harmless, or perversely exciting. The boys sometimes beat Agatha up, but she seemed never to bruise or scar.

Despite righteous anger at the terrible boys, and sympathy for Agatha, it was impossible not to taste their nasty gratification. Her very harmlessness invoked torturers. Being rich and pampered was already potentially offensive, but somehow luxurious gifts begged for cruelty. In our cramped, roach-infested apartment, she produced tales of abomination, lying on our couch in the smartest frock from the smartest shop. She had everything. Every pleasure, every pain. From smart shops to sleazy joints, the limp, colorless bit of girl burned along the extremest cutting edge of the sixties until her mother had her committed to a Manhattan madhouse. When Sylvia learned that it cost several hundred dollars a day, she was outraged.

We visited Agatha. She sat in a neat gray room with barred windows, high above the city, looking still softer and weaker, chastened into a quiet, spiritual composure. It was indeed a look. She loved it, so plain and pure and holy. It was even sexy, and it had been earned. It was really hers, not a designer's, nothing you'd ever see in a fashion magazine. She named many celebrities who had stayed in this hospital, and she described young people among the inmates who were marvelously interesting. She'd fallen among sensitive kids much like herself. Artists, really, not lunatics. We'd gone to the hospital feeling sorry for her, frightened by what we'd see. We came away annoyed, feeling foolish. She loved the place, was in no hurry to leave. She stayed about five weeks and came out a lesbian. She'd met and fallen in love with a wonderful crazy girl who treated her very badly.

§ In those days R. D. Laing and others sang praises to the condition of being nuts, and French intellectuals argued for allegiance to Stalin and the Marquis de Sade. Diane Arbus looked hard at freaks, searching maybe for a reservoir of innocence in this world. Lenny Bruce, at the Village Vanguard, a few blocks northwest of MacDougal Street, was doing hilarious self-immolating numbers. A few blocks east, at the Five Spot, Ornette Coleman eviscerated jazz essence through a raucous plastic sax. In salient forms of life and art, people exceeded themselves—or the self; our dashing President, John F. Kennedy, was screwing movie actresses. Everything dazzled.

Movies, the quintessence of excess, were becoming known as films. To a reflective eye, Antonioni's movies were among the most important. Sylvia and I never missed one. We'd emerge radically deadened, yet exhilarated, sorry that the movie had had to end. She whispered once, as the lights came on, "Why can't they leave us alone?" It was truly painful, having to thrust back into the windy streets, back to our apartment. We carried away visions of despair, exacerbated through relentless boredom toward thrilling apprehensions of this moment, in this modern world, where emptiness could be exquisite, even a way of life, not only for Monica Vitti and Alain Delon but for us, too. Why not? Besides, what else was there? We'd read Nietzsche. Our brainiest friends—not only sad little Agatha—brought regular news from the abyss. This one had become a junkie. That one strolled the wall beside the Hudson River, a willing prey to rough trade.

I'd come back to the apartment after shopping for groceries, or doing the laundry—Sylvia never did these things, never once—and find Agatha lying about, telling all. I could hardly wait to hear it from Sylvia, stories about the wilderness of Manhattan where Agatha descended nightly. When she stayed very late, I'd walk her down into the street, then wait with her for a cab. I worried about her. She might run into trouble—hapless, defenseless girl—alone in the dark. My heart, long nourished on latkes and gefilte fish, refused to acknowledge that she was actually running after trouble in the dark.

"It's too cold to wait out here."

"No bother. I want to do it."

I peered down the avenue, freezing, praying for a cab to appear and take Agatha away. Then I hurried back to Sylvia. Agatha had told her how a boy forced her into prostitution. He took her to a boat docked on the West Side, then down into a small room. He kept her there until the men came, bestial types. While one did things to her, others watched.

Repeating it to me—the boat, the small room, the men—Sylvia was ironically amused, posturing in her voice, mimicking Agatha's dull tones, as if to measure the distance between Agatha's lust for degrading experience and herself. I listened, feeling entertained without feeling guilty. I let myself imagine Agatha was far gone, object more than subject, without claims on my humanity. I owed only politeness. A few minutes in the street waiting for a cab. What sympathy I felt was easy. Liking her was also easy. Affectations, corrosive cosmetics, stylish clothes, an aura of self-destructive debauch—she was non-threatening, even sort of cute. I liked myself for liking her. She reported every peculiarity of her soul to Sylvia, but I didn't see, beneath Sylvia's contempt in retelling the stories, that she was involved in Agatha's fate. Then, one night in bed, Sylvia said, "Call me whore, slut, cunt . . ."

I was eventually to call her my wife. The old-fashioned name would make our life proper, okay. Things would change, I believed, though our fights had become so ugly and loud that the gay couple across the hall wouldn't ever say hello to us. We passed frequently, almost touching, along the dingy route to the hall toilets, one for each apartment, dank closets, a bowl, overhead tank, and a long chain. They turned up their phonograph until it boomed above our shrieking. Eighteenth-century pieces, wildly flourishing strings and an extravaganza of golden trumpets, as if to remind us of high, vigorous civilization where even the most destructive passions are sublimed. They hoped to drown us, maybe shame us, into silence. It never happened.

_____

It's possible we frightened them with our horrendous daily battles, but I assumed they just didn't like us. They were repressed Midwestern types. Towheaded, hyper-clean, quiet kids in flight from a Midwestern town, hiding in New York so they could be lovers, never supposing that their neighbors, just across the hall, would be maniacs. It struck me as paradoxical that being gay didn't mean you couldn't be disapproving and intolerant. I liked eighteenth-century music. Couldn't they tell? Forgive a little? Were their domestic dealings, because they behaved better, so different from ours? Sharing a bed, were they never deranged by sexual theatrics or loony compulsions? They passed us with rigid, wraith-like, blind faces. No hello, no little nod, only the sound of old linoleum crackling beneath our steps. They pressed toward the wall so as not to touch us inadvertently. We were an order of life beneath recognition. Their soaring music damned us. Their silence and their music threw me back on myself, made me think Sylvia and I—not the gay kids—were marginal creatures, morally offensive, in very bad taste. We were, but they seemed unjust. They really didn't know. I didn't either as I held Sylvia and called her names and said that I loved her. Didn't know we were lost.

§ Soon after we were married, Sylvia said, "I have girlfriends who make a hundred dollars a week," which was significant money in the early sixties. It would have

_____

paid two months' rent and our electric bills. But Sylvia only meant, compared to her girlfriends, I was a bum. I'd published a story or two in literary magazines that paid nearly nothing. So I began looking for a job, and I was soon hired as an assistant professor of English at Paterson State College in New Jersey. Then I stopped writing. I had much less time for stories, but the fact of being married changed my idea of myself. I now had to work for a living. I'd never believed that writing stories was work—it was merely hard. Besides, the sound of my typewriter, hour after hour, caused Sylvia pain. So did my family and friends. Whatever had importantly to do with me—family, friends, writing—shoved her to the margins of my consciousness, she thought, and she'd feel neglected and insulted. This also happened if I stayed in the hall toilet too long, and when we walked in the street. I'd be talking about a friend or a magazine article, maybe laughing, and I'd suppose that I was entertaining her, but then I'd notice she wasn't beside me. I'd look back. There she was, twenty feet behind, down the street, standing still, staring after me with rage. "You make me feel like a whore," she said. "Don't you dare walk ahead of me in the street." Then she walked past me and I trailed her home, very annoyed, but also wondering if there was something wrong with my personality, carrying on that way, talking and laughing, having a good time, as if I enjoyed being alive. That could seem an obnoxious innocence to other people. At the building door, Sylvia waited for me to arrive and open it, so that she'd feel properly treated, like a lady, not a whore.

She'd never say, "You're walking too fast. Please slow down." She'd slow down, lag behind, let me discover that I was treating her like a whore. It was hard, from moment to moment—walking, talking, laughing, writing, shitting—not to say or do something that hurt and infuriated Sylvia. I'd discover myself feeling apologetic, then angry for feeling apologetic.

The one time I got sick, I wanted only to go to sleep, but I felt apologetic for that, too. Still, I had to go to bed; sleep. I had a fever. I ached all over. It was only a cold, no big deal. But really, I had to lie down and sleep. The moment I shut my eyes, Sylvia began to sweep the floor around the bed. She decided I couldn't lie there, sick, surrounded by a filthy floor, though we had roaches, fleas, and sometimes rats in the apartment, and there were holes in the walls through which spilled brown, hairy, fibrous insulation. She swept with great force. Then she washed the dishes, making a racket, but everything had to be cleaned because I was sick. She put clothes away in drawers, slamming them shut, and hustled about picking things up, straightening the place. When the apartment was as clean as it could be, she said I couldn't lie on those sheets. We'd slept on them for several weeks and they were stained and dirty. I got out of bed and stood in my underwear, hot and shivering, while she changed the sheets. When she finished, I flopped back into the bed. I fell asleep, but was soon awakened by an unnatural silence. I saw Sylvia standing at the foot of the bed, staring at me, shifting her weight from side to side as if she had to pee. She looked frightened. "You're sick," she said. "You have to see a doctor. Get up. Don't lie there. Get up."

I said, "I come from peasant stock. Nothing can kill me."

"This isn't funny. Get up."

I got up, too sick to argue, and put on clothes. We walked eight or nine blocks, through the freezing night, to the emergency room at St. Vincent's, then waited in line with drug addicts and crazies. Eventually, I was seen by a doctor. He said I had a cold. I should go to bed. Two or three hours after I'd gone to bed, I went to bed. Sylvia felt much better. In the morning, I was well.

§ During the week, I rose at 5:30 a.m. and rode the subway to the Port Authority Bus Terminal, then took a bus to Paterson, then another to the college, where I struggled up a tall hill, icy in the winter, to the office I shared with everyone in the English department. I taught classes all day. Then I made the long trip back to MacDougal Street, where I found Sylvia waiting for me. She was in good spirits when she did well at school, and once was very happy. She'd been given a small scholarship. Other times she was in a deranged state, because she believed that I was fucking my students.

I once found her sprawled in a chair, shining with

perspiration. Drawers had been emptied, contents strewn about the apartment. The bed was overturned.

"All right," she said, "where is it?"

"Where is what?"

She laughed, tipping her head back arrogantly, as if to say I couldn't fool her. She meant, I slowly realized, that I'd hidden the evidence of my infidelity—love notes, nude photos of my girlfriends, etc. There was no such evidence. There were only my journals, but Sylvia never found them. We then had an argument that lasted until long after midnight. My crime, real only in her head, couldn't be disproved or ignored.

§ Bundled up and sweating in a heavy winter coat, my galoshes splashing in the sooty gray suck of New York snow, I lumbered down the empty, pre-dawn darkness of MacDougal Street toward the subway. My briefcase, fat with books and papers, bumped my leg. It was an ugly way to greet the morning, but I liked getting out of the apartment and I felt pretty good by the time I walked into the bus terminal. There was always a crowd of hats and coats, men packed together at the steamy breakfast counter, where other men sliced oranges with speed and grace, and served coffee and a variety of doughnuts. The steam carried good smells. I had my breakfast standing there, in a crowd of silent men huddled over orange juice, its taste bright as its color, or hot coffee, cup in one hand, cigarette in the other. Oppression lay in every face, but this was real, the hustle and crush of city action, the New York essence of it, the place to be.

I wasn't fucking my students, though I couldn't not see that some of the Italian girls, from towns in New Jersey, were visually delicious. At night, surrendering to fatigue, I exuded what was repressed in the classroom, like radioactive emissions of elemental decay. Then dusky Italian girls in Secaucus, Trenton, Paterson, and Jersey City sat up in moisture, gorgeous girls with olive skin and wavy hair, their eyes inflamed by the incubus of sexual torture. I never touched any of them. They had the handwriting of little children and drew bubbles over the letter *i*.

I had sex only with Sylvia, me coming without much pleasure, she without coming. Our electrical frenzy— contortions, convulsions, thrashing, vicious kissing— left us wiped out and horny, needing something other, something more. I yearned for it and I told myself I didn't need it and it wasn't important, though I looked at women in the subways and streets and my body said otherwise. This was my secret infidelity, feelings never confessed to my journals. Despite the insane daily misery of my marriage, I wrote that I loved Sylvia and wiped sincerely pathetic tears from my eyes, but to my shame, my body burned for the black woman in high heels and a tweed suit who stood near me one afternoon, while waiting for the D train at the West Fourth Street station, and the woman who drove by in a silver Porsche at the corner of West Fourth and MacDougal, and the young

Puerto Rican mother carrying a shopping bag, who looked so weary. In seconds these women were imprinted in my nerves and bones, though I never said a word to them, never saw them again. I remembered them with despair.

In the spring of 1963, after Sylvia completed her undergraduate work at N.Y.U., we moved uptown to an apartment near Columbia. She took night classes in German. I continued teaching at Paterson State, and I joined a car pool, which made the trip easier. I'd come home less exhausted. After a while, I tried to write again. Another story or two ended up in obscure literary magazines.

§ We acquired a group of new friends who taught at Columbia. They often came by at night, and sometimes we sat talking and smoking marijuana until dawn. Our conversations were usually about literature or movies, and were much influenced by marijuana, hence very thrilling, but also very boring. As in Antonioni's movies, there was weird gratification in the boredom of our long, smoky, moribund-hip, analytical nights. Sylvia, the only woman in the room, loved every minute. She'd pull her legs up on the couch and half lie there, looking languid and vibrant, and was soon helpless with marijuana giggles, laughing at herself for laughing so much, unable to stop, and the others would laugh with her, encouraging her too much, I thought. But they had nothing at stake. Sylvia's susceptibility to marijuana was amusing, even endearing, to everyone but me. I feared and resented these moments, and I despised dope. I never bought any, but it was always in the apartment. Friends "laid" it on us, joints and pills, in return for our hospitality. Once, returning from the grocery with a bag of food pressed to my chest, I passed an acquaintance who, saying hello, dropped some hashish cubes into the bag. Dopers always proselytized and were always generous. Too generous with Sylvia. I never bought, and because it might seem rude, I never said no. I'd put the joints and pills in a drawer. Weeks later, when I came upon the stuff by accident, I'd throw it out.

The long conversational nights were also full of academic gossip about the English department at Columbia. Our friends knew they were going to be fired, since it was the department's tradition to fire people, but they weren't absolutely sure when it would happen, or if, by some miracle, the department would choose to keep them. They were saved from nervous breakdowns by the hope of being among the chosen, lots of marijuana, downers, uppers, and occasionally heroin. Eventually they lay before senior colleagues who, like ancient Mayan priests, cut out their hearts. To their credit, they tried to destroy themselves first with drugs.

I was afraid that marijuana would intensify Sylvia's paranoia, and I pleaded with her not to smoke it unless I was there with her. She'd hide cigarettes and pills that were given to her. Sometimes she'd confess that she'd smoked when I was out. I'd become outraged, I'd make puritanical scenes, but I wasn't consistent. If she smoked, I smoked. If she took pills, I did, too. It was a way of being close, and as everyone knows, dope makes sex dreamier and longer, when it doesn't just kill desire.

§ We spent a three-day weekend in the apartment, eating speed, smoking grass, and reading and rereading *The Turn of the Screw*, for the evil feeling in this disgusting masterpiece. We didn't answer the phone, hardly ate, and we had bouts of hard, compulsive sex, after which we lay there aching for more. Toward the end of the third day, Sylvia began saying, "Open the window," as if it were a marvelous little poem:

> *O*–pen.
> *The win*–dow.

I asked her to stop, but she repeated it about a thousand times, in singsong tones, before collapsing beside me in a stupor, and then she told me what *The Turn of the Screw* is really about, going on and on, both of us overwhelmed by her luminous ravings, though we didn't remember any of it later.

In the conversational style of the day, everything was always *about* something; or everything was always *really about* something else. A halo of implication lifted like shimmering gas *about* innocuous words, movies, faces, and events reported in newspapers. The plays and sonnets of Shakespeare and the songs of Dylan were all equally *about* something. The murder of President Kennedy was, too. Nothing was fully resident in itself. Nothing was plain.

Stoned on grass or opium or bennies or downers, lying side by side in our narrow bed as streetlights came on, we'd follow their patterns on the walls and ceiling as we listened to late-night radio talk shows. Our favorite was Long John Nebel. One night a caller said, in a languorous, ignorant drawl, "Long John, you have missed the whole boat." Naked in our drugged radio darkness, we turned to each other with a rush of gluey love and happiness. For months thereafter, we said affectionately, "You have missed the whole boat." Sylvia was sometimes high-spirited and funny, but it is easier to remember the bad times. They were more frequent and sensational; also less painful now than remembering what I loved.

§ At the end of my school year, I resigned from my job at Paterson State, reapplied to graduate school at Michigan, and began to audit summer-school classes at Columbia to recover the feel of lectures and the formal study of literature. There were more fights with Sylvia, but we were clear about the idea that I was going to leave. I said I would leave.

—

§ The train from Grand Central to Ann Arbor, Michigan, was called *The Wolverine.* The trip took ten hours, from dark to dawn. In the long, clattering night, hungry, unable to sleep, I opened the paper bag of sandwiches, cookies, and coffee that Sylvia had prepared for me. She hadn't ever done anything like that before. Now that we were separating, I'd been unable to stop her. When I unscrewed the aluminum cap of the thermos bottle, a small folded paper fell out. I opened it and read a penciled note from Sylvia: *I love you.*

She loves me, I thought, and nothing more, as blackness hurtled by in the window, interrupted by tiny piercing distant single lights and clusters of lights, like stars. I ate everything in the bag and drank all the coffee. I smoked until I felt only the heat and tear of cigarette devastations in my throat.

§ A few weeks passed before Sylvia decided to join me in Michigan. Her decision was impulsive and sentimental. I didn't object. I missed her. I never looked at my journals and I remembered none of the small, mean, daily miseries that were the texture of our life. I could remember if I tried, but I didn't try. I didn't think. I was very happy to see her when she got off the train, her black bangs and bright black eyes. She was smiling at me, walking toward me with an exaggerated side-to-side, fat-kid, rocking motion, being silly to show her happiness.

—

Our fights began again in Michigan and were as bad as those in New York. One night she stood at the bathroom mirror and methodically smashed at her reflection with a metal ashtray, the glass streaking and flashing out of the frame. She said:

"You *(smash)* don't *(smash)* love *(smash)* me *(smash)*. But you will miss me."

I helped her pack and I took her to the train station. Though anxious and depressed, we didn't fight. We were, instead, very affectionate. This was it. The end. She returned to New York, and then I was wretched in a whole new way, because I wasn't really wretched and I felt guilty about that. I wrote to her and phoned her frequently.

On visits to New York during school vacations, I stayed with Sylvia in her new apartment on Sullivan Street, which was much like the one on MacDougal Street, hardly more than a room. We made love again, in our manner, as if we still desired to make real whatever it was that bound us to each other. Before my last visit, Christmas vacation, 1964, Sylvia returned to the apartment near Columbia, which she had sublet while living on Sullivan Street. I went to New York with the intention of talking to her about a divorce. We'd never mentioned divorce, and I didn't know how to bring it up.

§ Shortly before we separated the first time, a few weeks before I left for Michigan, she'd said very obliquely that other men would be interested in her. I said, "I'm sure you'll have no trouble finding somebody when I'm gone," assuming that was what she wanted to hear. Instantly, she flew at me, tearing at my face. I swatted her hands reflexively, with a sidewise motion, and, by accident, must have brushed her nose. She shrieked, "You broke my nose," and lunged at the living-room window, ripping through the slats of the blinds and shrieking for the police. She mutilated the slats but didn't manage to open the window, and she was still shrieking, "Police, police, help," as I dragged her away from the window and tried to hold her and take a look at her nose. She pushed me back and dashed into the bathroom. Leaning over the sink, she stared closely at her face in the mirror, saying, "It's broken. Look." It looked no different.

I hadn't felt my hand touch her nose, but I apologized again and again and I studied her nose carefully, respectfully. In her mind she had a broken nose and I had broken it. That was the point. She stayed at the mirror a long time, slowly turning her face this way and that, an excited glow in her eyes, like an artist studying a piece of work with quiet satisfaction.

Finally, in a mood of strained reconciliation, we went out to find a doctor. Our apartment was only a block from West End Avenue, where the ground floor of many buildings was given over to the offices of doctors, dentists, and psychiatrists. We rang a bell. A doctor answered, and agreed to look at Sylvia's nose right then. It was late afternoon. There happened to be no patients in his waiting room. He touched Sylvia's nose, pressing lightly on one side, then the other. Glancing at me, he said with gentle, mock dismay, "He didn't do it, did he?"

Sylvia said, "No. He's too nice."

The doctor said he didn't think her nose was broken. Sylvia asked if he would refer her to a specialist.

"What kind of specialist?"

"I want a plastic surgeon."

I guessed what she had in mind. Fixing the broken nose might be an opportunity to shorten her nose.

The plastic surgeon's office was on Park Avenue. There were well-dressed women in his waiting room, one or two with bandaged noses. There were no magazines, only photo albums showing former patients before and after plastic surgery, their noses much shortened. Nostril holes stood up and gaped at you like a second pair of eyes.

The surgeon's receptionist and two nurses had noses like the ones in the photos—Pekingese snouts—his mark, his vision, his ego-ideal. All these women, it seemed, wanted to please the surgeon. It was inconceivable that they'd pleased themselves. I thought to warn Sylvia against the man, but she hadn't yet decided to have surgery and it might have caused a dispute in the waiting room.

When one of the nurses called Sylvia, I went, too. I felt uncomfortable being there, but she wanted me along. I followed her through a room divided into half a dozen curtained stalls, where the surgeon saw postoperative patients, perhaps five or six per hour. He received us in his office, a big, thick-chested man with a mangled-looking, heavy, Jewish face, a huge nose, and a voice that seemed to rumble at us through a sewer pipe.

Sylvia talked shyly about her broken nose, saying not a word about surgery. I supposed she had been shaken by the photo albums. As she talked, the surgeon stared, anticipating how he could chop. She was hesitant, smiling pitifully, and said only that she thought her nose might be broken. It didn't look quite straight. Perhaps something could be done.

He told Sylvia to sit on a stool, then stood before her, cupped the back of her head with both hands, and pulled her face toward him, gradually mashing her nose against his belly, harder and harder, holding it there for about ten seconds. Then he released her. His fee was a hundred dollars. We paid and never discussed the incident.

This was the consequence of my saying she'd have no trouble finding somebody after I left. To talk about a divorce might result in a far greater enormity. But I had to talk about divorce. We'd been living separate lives for over a year. I'd been seeing another woman. I didn't know if Sylvia was seeing other men. She intimated things on the telephone, but was always so vague that, without sounding crazed by jealousy, I couldn't ask if she was telling me that she was fucking somebody. I didn't want to hear about it. She did the best she could,

I suppose, to be honest. Neither of us had the courage to speak plainly.

In New York, near the end of my vacation, December 30, 1964, I went to meet her. I was determined to talk about a divorce.

§ I don't remember if I picked her up at the apartment or if we met in a restaurant. I was very surprised to find another man present, Sylvia's "friend." He was blond and French, with a sensuously handsome face. I assumed he was no friend. With him in the picture, talking about a divorce might be no problem. Sylvia herself might bring it up.

At some point in the evening, Sylvia said good night to him. I don't remember that he and I said good night to each other. He was just no longer at the table. I was surprised again, having expected that Sylvia would say good night to me, not him. The friend gone, Sylvia and I walked to the apartment. The New York New Year's Eve celebration had begun early. There was garbage everywhere. Streets splattered with vomit looked strewn with hideous blazing flowers.

I felt as if nothing had really changed between us. We were together, walking home as we had many times. The familiarity of the moment, the ordinariness and naturalness of our being together, made me anxious. I had to talk about divorce, and I wanted to, but the subject seemed utterly incongruous and irrelevant. The mood was all wrong. I didn't feel angry or bitter. There was no feeling in me that could usher the subject into words. I told Sylvia that I would be taking my preliminary exams in two weeks. She said a little about her civil-service job. At the apartment, she changed into a short gray cotton nightgown and poured herself a glass of bourbon. She joined me on the living-room couch, lying on her back with her head in my lap. She talked, addressing the air above, not my face. I noticed a black cat in the apartment. It skulked about and had a broken tail, shaped like a flattened Z, or a lightning bolt.

Sylvia told me about men she'd been seeing in the past several months. Some were my friends. She let me know that she'd been sleeping with them by telling me little gossipy stories.

"He found out I was seeing his colleague and was very jealous. He said, 'Now I know what Othello feels like.' "

Her tone was amused and blasé, as if none of this could be painful to me. She went on for a long time, quite comfortable reviewing her affairs while lying with her head in my lap. I listened without saying a word. Her French friend, I supposed, had been an object lesson, or an introduction to what she planned to say when we were alone. She was mildly theatrical, stopping occasionally to lift her head and take another sip of bourbon. When the glass was empty, she refilled it, then went on about this one and that one.

About an hour passed with me not saying a word, but very miserable, locked in my old psychological prison, wondering if I'd ever feel good again. She'd given me plenty of reason to bring up divorce, to say very simply that I wanted a divorce, but she was doing all the talking, sipping her bourbon, gaily confessing her infidelities. The moment belonged to her. I could say nothing at all. Then she asked, "Would you like to try once more?" She meant resume our life in Michigan, while I completed my work for the Ph.D. The question stunned me. I hadn't expected anything like it, and yet I should have known it was coming, and that all the talk about other men was a preface to her question.

At the moment, I didn't think any of this. She seemed a different person, no longer the shy, hysterically explosive, paranoiac Sylvia, the one who was attractive to men and yet felt she was repulsive. This Sylvia was a glamorous, intellectual whore, flaunting her adventures in love, then asking if I'd like to have her back, as if she'd proved herself ravishingly depraved, brilliant in destructive spirit, and therefore very desirable. I was bloated by misery, heavy, stupid, burning. She'd said enough. She waited for my answer.

"Wait till I finish my exams. Then come to Ann Arbor."

She heard me. I said it clearly. I'd never felt worse.

Sylvia lay still for a while, weighing my words. Then she sat up and walked into the bedroom. I continued to sit on the couch, unable to think or talk, a dummy. Then she reappeared, stood at the end of the couch, and said, "I just swallowed forty-seven Seconals." She looked at my eyes. A flat look of that's that, and there you have it.

I said, "You're kidding."

She walked away to the bathroom. I stayed where I was, seated on the couch, not believing her, not disbelieving, and then I heard her groan. Her body fell to the floor, which is how it sounds. It does not sound like anything else. I hurried to the bathroom. She was sprawled on the tiles, underpants around one ankle. Apparently she'd fallen off the bowl while sitting on it. I dragged her to the couch, shouting at her, slapping her face, shaking her, and then I tried to walk her around the living room. I stopped only to phone the police, then went back to the bathroom, picked up her underpants, and pulled them up her legs. I tried again to make her walk, hooking her left arm around my shoulder, my right arm about her waist. It was no use. I was dragging her, not walking her. I dropped her back on the couch, straddled her, and pleaded and shouted while shaking her and furiously rubbing her wrists. I thought to make her vomit, but she was unconscious and I was afraid she would choke. Minutes later, two policemen entered the apartment. They did the same thing with Sylvia that I'd been doing, walking her about. Then there was an ambulance in the street. We carried her downstairs. I got into the ambulance with her. We shot across town to Knickerbocker Hospital, in Spanish Harlem.

A medical team was waiting to receive Sylvia. They went to work in an efficient, military way. I saw them cup her mouth with a respirator, then somebody asked me and the two policemen not to stand so close. We retreated to the doorway. As if I weren't there, one policeman said to the other, "She won't make it."

It had been less than half an hour since she fell. She was healthy; only twenty-four years old. It was impossible that she could just die, regardless of the liquor and pills, but I was scared and I thought in a simplistic way. She'd always been right about everything. I'd always been wrong. I loved her. I couldn't live without her. She'd proved it. I was convinced. No more proof was necessary, only that she open her eyes and live. I'd be what she liked. I'd do what she wanted. She'd know that I loved her and always had.

One of the medical staff asked me if I knew what Sylvia had swallowed. I told him what she said. He said they must do a tracheotomy. Sylvia wasn't breathing. But no one there had authority to perform a surgical procedure. All had foreign accents, Spanish and German. Perhaps they weren't yet fully licensed to practice medicine in America. I didn't understand why they were standing around, suddenly doing nothing. I urged the one who spoke to me to do the tracheotomy. I said, "Please do it." I begged. He was frightened. Another doctor appeared, wearing street clothes, coming down the hall, walking briskly to the exit. He was a pale, strong-boned man. He looked authoritative, like a hero or a god, as if he could perform surgery, climb a mountain, kill people, anything. The one who'd spoken to me,

a short dark Spanish doctor—if he was a doctor—
stopped him, explaining the situation in a pleading tone.
With a gesture of disgust, the godlike doctor brushed
him aside and went out the door. The Spanish doctor
then returned to Sylvia. The others stood about the
table, grimly watching as he performed the tracheotomy.
I watched from the doorway, forbidden to step closer.
The Spanish doctor was taking a chance with his career
and his life. At least that's what I thought. With everything to lose, he did the job.

Moments later he turned to me and said Sylvia would
be all right. He was pleased, happy, assuring. She was
breathing normally. They wheeled her away to a room
upstairs. I followed and sat beside the bed. I told her we
would go to Michigan, and that I wished she would open
her eyes. She didn't open her eyes, didn't move.

I left the room to phone family and friends. Some
arrived in the middle of the night, some early the next
morning. Things were said. A little registered on me:

"I feel terrible. I never visited her. She would call me
sometimes."

"She was always a neurotic. I don't know why he
married her."

"Is she getting the best possible attention? I want to
call in another doctor."

"Get the key to her apartment. We should investigate,
find out what she took. We'll need her medical insurance
papers. I believe she had a cat. Has somebody fed the
cat?"

Sylvia didn't wake, but she continued breathing normally. Her face turned once in my direction, as if her mind was alert, taking in my presence through flat, thick, general, insensate immobility. I held her hand and smoothed her hair, but mainly just sat by the bed. Now and then I left the room and dozed in the hall, on a wooden bench.

For two nights and days, I slept on the bench and sat with Sylvia, afraid to leave the hospital before she woke up. It seemed too dangerous to leave; too unlucky, too risky. The Spanish doctor drew me into an office the second or third day. He said again Sylvia would recover. It was a medical miracle, he said, but I mustn't expect too much. She'd been unconscious for a long time. No telling if she had suffered brain damage. "She might no longer be the person you remember." I didn't believe she'd suffered brain damage.

During the third night, as I slept outside her room, I was awakened by terrible shouts in a German accent— "Seel-vya"—and the sound of hard slaps. I looked into the room. The heroic doctor who had refused to do the tracheotomy was bent over her, shouting her name and slapping her face, as if she were a very disobedient child who wouldn't wake up. He had been bad-tempered and dismissive. Now he was angry at her. I pitied him, but I hated him, too, and wished him ill. Sylvia didn't open her eyes.

The next morning I went downstairs and sat in a reception area. A black man and two women, perhaps his wife and his sister, stood waiting there. They were nicely dressed, as if to show respect for the hospital. The Spanish doctor appeared. As he walked toward them, his face opened with expectation, like their faces. For an instant it seemed that he was about to receive news from them. But it was he who spoke:

"Your daughter died. I am so sorry."

I then understood his expression. He'd imitated what he saw in their faces, their expectation, to show that he felt as they did. But it was instinctive; he wasn't deliberately showing anything; he was simply feeling what they did. The black gentleman said, "She only fell down the stairs." The women embraced each other and cried, and then the man cried. I felt sorry for all of them and for me.

I restrained my own tears. The thought came to me that there had been a sacrifice. A woman had died. Sylvia would wake up. Too bad it had to be this way, but in God's scheme of things, there is terrible justice. Sylvia and I would soon be leaving the hospital.

I thought, If I were rich, I'd give a fortune to this hospital for the many who would receive its care, and the many who would cry. I was afloat on dreams of myself as a seer and an immensely generous benefactor, and though I was sure I could run a fast mile or lift great weights if necessary, I was very tired. Somebody found me wandering about. I was told to go home, Sylvia would be all right. I could go home, take a shower, change my clothes. I left the hospital. It was okay to shower.

When I got out of the shower, the phone rang. It was the hospital. They told me to come back. I dressed quickly, ran out, found a taxi. As I entered the hospital, I was stopped at the desk. There had been a phone call from my brother. A nurse told me to return the call before going to Sylvia's room. She insisted. I phoned. My brother answered. He said Sylvia had died. The nurse waited outside the phone booth. She told me to go now to Sylvia's room, collect her things. My feet walked to her room. I didn't remember what things I was supposed to collect. I saw a clean, white, empty bed. I saw emptiness. I left the hospital with nothing, nothing at all.